A Message for McCleod

Tom McCleod, relentlessly pursued by three riders, learns that a young woman he once knew has disappeared. Where is Sandy Kruger? Riding with the outcast Cherokee George, McCleod sets out on the quest to find her.

Can Sandy herself survive? She is one woman against the wilderness. And to make matters worse, she is being hunted by a merciless gang of gunslicks led by the owner of the Cinch Buckle, the very ranch from which she has escaped. McCleod will need his wits and his guns as the dangerous trail unwinds towards the final encounter. There are secrets to be revealed, but will McCleod find Sandy in time?

By the same author

Last Reckoning for the Presidio Kid
Payback at Black Valley Forge

A Message for McCleod

Emmett Stone

ROBERT HALE · LONDON

First published in Great Britain 2012

ISBN 978-0-7090-9262-9

Robert Hale Limited
Clerkenwell House
Clerkenwell Green
London EC1R 0HT

www.halebooks.com

Typeset by
Derek Doyle & Associates, Shaw Heath
Printed and bound in Great Britain by
CPI Antony Rowe, Chippenham and Eastbourne

CHAPTER ONE

McCleod drew the chestnut Morgan to a halt and dismounted. He reached into his saddle-bags for his field glasses and put them to his eyes. The three riders were still there. His best efforts so far to shake them off had failed. He had tried doubling and changing direction. He had ridden through streams and watercourses, to no avail. There was something relentless about the way they kept following him. His horse was tired. It was his spare horse. He had ridden the first one almost into the ground before leaving him in the charge of the livery man at Low Butte. Somewhere along the line those three had exchanged mounts too. The horses they were riding now were paints, rangy and tough. They would keep going for a long time. He looked closely at the riders but there was nothing much he could see. Two of them appeared to be bearded. All three had their bandannas pulled up high and their Stetsons pulled low. They were giving nothing away. Even their clothes were ordinary and nondescript. Only one thing about them was unusual: they just kept right on coming.

His eyes swept the broken landscape ahead of him. There was prickly pear, juniper and stunted pine. He was getting into canyon country. Heat waves made the air shimmer and a heavy silence hung over everything. High in the air a buzzard soared and a lizard moved across the sand at his feet. Far ahead of him, across the burning desert, reared the long high edge of the Buffalo tablelands. He hadn't intended going that way but it seemed to offer a good chance of finally shaking off his pursuers. He knew the country a little; not well, but perhaps better than they did. It was worth a try.

He placed the glasses back into their case and mounted up. Between him and the Buffalo plateau the land was virtually dry, but he knew a few places that might have water, places with which his pursuers would be unfamiliar. At least, he had to hope they would be. His horse was already tired so he let it walk slowly. That way there was the added advantage that it raised no dust. Not that he was hopeful of easily giving the slip to his pursuers. Days of having them follow him had persuaded him of that. Maybe one of them was a tracker. He began to search his memory once again, trying to figure who would want to follow him so doggedly. Until recently he had been working for a railroad company, providing buffalo meat for the construction workers. He could think of nothing untoward that had happened while he had been doing that job. He thought about his recent past and then tried to reach further back in time. He had done a lot of things apart from buffalo hunting. He had been a prospector, a bronc buster, a lumberjack, a flatboat man, even done some land surveying along the Mexican border. Sure, he had made enemies; any man did. But he could think of nothing which would account for his present situation.

It was late the following afternoon and the sun was about to drop quickly behind the western skyline when McCleod reached the creek bed he had in mind. It was dry. He had water left in his canteen; he took a sip and gave some to the Morgan. He looked back across the desert he had ridden but this time there was no sign of his pursuers. He knew, however, that they were still somewhere behind him. He considered making camp for the night but decided against it. The air was still heavy with heat. It was another twenty miles to the next waterhole. After allowing time for the horse to recuperate, he climbed into leather and started riding as the sun vanished and stars swam up into the sky.

The night was still. McCleod knew how cold it could get, but for the moment he was grateful for the coolness. Weird shapes loomed out of the darkness; cactus plants held out supplicating arms like tattered beggars. After a time the Morgan grew restive. Its ears pricked and McCleod peered anxiously about. This was Apache country; he guessed the Morgan had picked up the scent of an Indian pony. Instinctively, he touched the Winchester residing in its scabbard but the Morgan soon recovered its equilibrium and continued plodding on, its hoofs making no noise in the desert sand. When he figured that he had put enough space between himself and his pursuers, McCleod finally brought the horse to a halt and made camp for the rest of the night.

He was up early next morning. Before long the sun had turned the desert into a shimmering fantasy of heat and dancing mirages. He had used up the last of his water and knew that if the next waterhole was dry, he was in deep trouble. Before long his throat felt parched and his head began to ache. He felt confused. He couldn't be sure that he was on the right track. Then he saw what he was looking for; a patch of brush which indicated the presence of water. He spurred the weary Morgan up a slight slope and slid from the saddle. If there had been water, the Morgan would have smelled it. Already McCleod knew the worst. The waterhole was dry. He fell to the ground, his face in the sand, till the nuzzling of the Morgan aroused him. He stood up and began to walk towards the bushes. When he had found what he thought was an appropriate spot, he got down on his hands and knees and began to dig, scooping sand with a desperation that soon became almost a frenzy. Sweat was pouring from him and flies buzzed around his head in a cloud. He stopped for a moment and then carried on scooping until he was rewarded by a faint dampness in the sand. With renewed vigour he carried on digging until he had made a substantial hole which began to fill with a brackish liquid. Laughing to himself, McCleod sucked up the dirty water, not caring how it tasted. When he had finished he let the Morgan drink and then he sat back, built a smoke and lay in the shelter of a rock while he contemplated what his next move should be.

The Buffalo tableland wasn't too far ahead of him. He decided that his best course of action would be to carry on and ride up into the mesa. From there he would have a clear view over his back trail. He would be able to tell whether his pursuers were still on his tail or whether the exigencies of the desert had been too much for them. If they were still there, he would be in a good position to deal with them once and for all. Getting to his feet, he did the best he could to fill his canteen and then stepped into the saddle. As the Morgan moved on, his eyes continued to watch for any signs of danger. He wasn't too worried about the Apache but it didn't hurt to be cautious. Sweat rolled down his back and bathed his body under his shirt. He felt stale. The body of the Morgan, too, was darkened and stained. It would be good to reach higher ground.

As he approached the mesa, McCleod began to pick out some of the details. Its red tinted walls stood over a thousand feet high and seemed impregnable till he perceived that the sheer face was broken at several points by deep canyons that wound back into the rock. Selecting one of these, McCleod rode into it. Narrow at first, it soon opened out to form a deep valley with sloping sides. The trail was well marked and rose gradually. After the heat and dust of the desert, the air felt mild and balmy and McCleod drew it in with deep satisfaction. Riding in this way for some time, he found another canyon. It was narrower and steeper but seemed to offer a quicker route to the top of the mesa. The horse picked its way carefully but eventually McCleod got down and walked beside it. Finally he hobbled the animal and went on foot the rest of the way. When he reached the top he had a perfect view over the desert. He sat down beneath a wind-blasted pinon, built himself a smoke, and prepared to wait.

It was next morning he saw them. He had camped for the night where he had left the horse and returned to the summit with the dawn. He was beginning to think that he must have succeeded in throwing his pursuers off his trail when, through his field glasses, he saw a smudge in the distance which he knew was the dust from their horses. It wasn't Apache; they would leave no such obvious trail. Putting down the field glasses, he continued to sit for a time. Drawing out the makings, he rolled himself a cigarette. A breeze was blowing over the top of the mesa but the sun was warm. Down there on the desert floor it would soon be stifling. When he had finished the smoke he put the field glasses to his eyes again. Now he could make out the three riders. They must have a tracker, he thought, and cursed out loud. Then he got to his feet and made his way decisively down the slope of the hill to where he had left the Morgan. Mounting up, he rode through the canyon up to its junction with the valley trail. He jumped down, tethered the horse where no one would detect it and selected a spot behind some boulders overlooking the trail. Maybe his pursuers would be prepared for an ambush, but it was a chance he was willing to take. He had had enough of the whole damned situation. He checked the Winchester and his six-guns and then sat back to await the arrival of his unwitting guests.

Time passed. He could have done with another cigarette. Occasionally he took a sip of water from the canteen he had filled with fresh water from a runnel. He kept his eyes fixed on the trail leading up to his place of concealment. He had a good view. He supposed they were just being cautious. It was just a matter of keeping patience. It was only when he heard the click of a rifle being levelled behind him that he knew he had been outmanoeuvred.

'Don't make a move!'

The voice came from above and behind him.

'We have you covered. Just do as I say and you might come out of this alive.'

McCleod was tempted to turn his head but felt it might be more advisable under the circumstances to follow his instruction to the letter.

'Now, throw aside the rifle and the gunbelt.'

McCleod did as he was ordered. He heard the sound of boots and a pair of legs came into his vision as somebody stooped and picked up the weapons.

'All right, you can turn round now. But do it real slow and don't think of tryin' any tricks.'

Very carefully, McCleod moved his body. Standing on a rock was a man with a rifle pointed at his chest. To his right and a little apart stood a second man with a rifle; a third man was standing to his left holding the weapons McCleod had discarded. He had seen enough through his field glasses to recognize them as his pursuers. Two of them wore beards; the third was clean-shaven and looked like a Mexican. They all wore range clothes that were caked with dirt and sweat.

'What's this all about?' McCleod said.

He was angry with himself for having been outwitted. The three men must have entered the mesa by another canyon entrance and then found a way to come up behind him. He should have been more alert. Looking at the three of them, he had a feeling that it was the clean-shaven Mexican-looking *hombre* who was responsible for the tracking. He had certainly done a good job.

The two men who were standing higher up the slope moved down and he was able to get a closer look at their features. He saw now that the one who seemed to be their leader was quite considerably older than the other one and looked a lot meaner. The younger man stepped forward and began to frisk him.

'A little precaution,' the man who had spoken resumed. 'Just in case you happen to have anything else concealed about you.'

The man doing the frisking stood up.

'He's clean,' he said.

'What did you expect to find?' McCleod replied. 'A Gatling?'

'Maybe a knife or even a derringer.'

The speaker did not seem to notice the irony in McCleod's tone. He nodded to the others and they lowered their rifles.

'I think we could all do with some coffee,' he said. 'And this is good a spot as any. Mr McCleod, won't you be seated?'

McCleod sat down again. Presently the men had a fire going and a blackened pot of coffee boiling on the flames. The younger bearded man offered McCleod his pouch of tobacco. McCleod was about to refuse and say he had his own but changed his mind and accepted the offer. He might as well get something out of the situation. By the time he had taken a few drags and was on his second cup of coffee, he was feeling a little bit more relaxed.

'Let us introduce ourselves,' the leader resumed.

'You seem to know my name already,' McCleod said.

The man nodded.

'We do indeed. You are Tom McCleod. I am Carl Fogle.'

He pointed at the younger man.

'This gentleman is Roy Bunce and the other gentleman goes by the name of Cherokee George.'

Bunce's mouth twitched in acknowledgment but the features of Cherokee George remained inscrutable.

'He the one led you two through the desert?' McCleod said.

Fogle nodded.

'Mr George is part Indian. He has skills which, unfortunately, we lack. He is indeed responsible for getting us here.'

'You two payin' him?'

'Yes, and paying him well. There is a reason.'

'It had better be a good one,' McCleod replied.

He looked again at Cherokee George. He didn't look the sort who would be too concerned about money. Maybe if there was a lot of it.

'Mr McCleod,' Fogle resumed. 'Can you remember ever working for an outfit called the Hog Eye?'

McCleod thought hard.

'Sure,' he said. 'Down in the San Catrudos River country.'

'That's the one. Big spread. It was owned by a man called Kruger.'

'Yeah, sure. I remember him. Ran an efficient operation. Not too sure about the man himself.'

'Well, he now owns a ranch not too far from here called the Cinch Buckle.'

'Interestin', but so what?'

'Maybe you remember his daughter, a young woman name of Sandra.'

'Of course. Folks called her Sandy. She'd be about sixteen when I was workin' down there. She was a nice kid.'

'That'd be right. She's nineteen now. Leastways, if she ain't come to no harm.'

McCleod was suddenly interested.

'What do you mean, if she's not come to any harm?'

'The young lady disappeared. That's when I got involved. I had experience with the Texas Rangers.'

'Kind of a long way from Texas,' McCleod remarked.

'Yeah. I traced the young lady to a place called Cobb Corner.'

'Know it. Ain't no place for a lady.'

'Miss Kruger had found work in a general store.'

Bunce leaned across the fire.

'That's where I come in. Miss Kruger was stayin' with some friends of mine. I met the young lady a few times.'

'Did you start courtin' her?'

'I wouldn't exactly put it in those terms. I saw her a few times at my friends' house. We'd just sit on the porch and kinda chew things over. She seemed to be setllin' well. Then one day I went round and she wasn't there. None of us thought too much about it but when it turned out she'd left the general store in a hurry, we started to get worried. The folks she was stayin' with had seen her the night before. That was the last any of us saw of her.'

'What did you do about it?'

'Why, once we realized she wasn't around, we got up a party and set out to look for her, but we didn't find anything.'

'What, nothin' at all?'

'Nothing. She just seemed to have vanished. We kept hopin' she might come back.'

'Maybe you just didn't look hard enough.'

'That's when I arrived,' Fogle interjected. 'Like I say, I traced her to Cobb Corner but I got there just too late.'

McCleod finished his second cup of coffee.

'I don't see what this has to do with me,' he said.

Fogle reached into an inside pocket and produced a sheet of paper.

'Take a look at this,' he said.

McCleod took it.

'It's a letter. And it's meant for you.'

'It was found in her room,' Bunce added.

McCleod began to read.

Dear Mr McCleod,

I don't know where you are and it is unlikely I will ever find out so you will probably never get to read this. I am writing it to you all the same. Maybe you won't even remember me. I liked you from the moment you came to the ranch and started working for Mr Kruger. You were the only one who treated me like an intelligent person and not just a kid or something to leer at. Oh yes, I had plenty of that from some of the others. But you were different. Remember how I showed you one of my poems and you looked at it and said you thought it was good? You asked me if it was about something personal because it seemed all made up, and I said that it was but I'd tried not to make that too obvious. You said you thought I had a real talent and I showed you some of my favourite places for writing.

There was a new horse – remember? I called him Concho. You showed me how to break him in, not like some of the others did it, but gentle like. I was very sad the day you left, although I tried not to show it. Anyway, I decided to leave the ranch. I don't want to go into all the reasons for my decision. I won't say where I am at present – yes I will – it's a place called

Cobb Corner. I am working in a clothing emporium but I don't know how long I will stay here.

Here is a poem I wrote for you. Remember what I said about trying not to be too obvious.

Beneath the lilac
Against the wall,
At the foot of the garden -
The abandoned ball.

Phantoms flit
Across the lawn;
Some tattered leaves
The wind has torn.

While from a branch
Of the shadowed beech
The pale moon hangs
Just out of reach.

The child's asleep:
Now nothing seems
Quite so real
As in his dreams.

I don't really know about beech trees, but sometimes I think my dreams are the realest things in my life.

McCleod finished reading the letter.
'Is that it?' he said.
'There were a couple of loose papers. Nothin' in

particular. Doodles and stuff like that.'

McCleod lit another cigarette to cover his reaction to reading the letter and the poem. He had got on with the kid but this. . . .

'And what's your angle on my role in all this?' he finally said.

Bunce looked a little uncomfortable.

'To be honest, at first I thought you might know something about Miss Sandy's disappearance. From the Cinch Buckle, that is.'

'You mean you suspected me of bein' involved?'

'Not exactly that. Anyway, I soon changed my mind.'

'Now why would that be?'

Cherokee George had been a spectator of the conversation but there was a sudden movement from his direction.

'Because I put him right,' he said.

McCleod looked at him more closely.

'Do I know you?' he said.

'Nope. But I've heard your name mentioned from time to time.'

'Nice to have your endorsement,' McCleod replied.

'Mr McCleod,' Fogle said. 'Please don't misunderstand us. The reason we've been tracking you is that we feel you might be able to help in our search. Once we saw that letter, we figured you would want to be involved.'

McCleod poured another cup of coffee.

'You coulda made contact with me before this,' he

said. 'I waited around in Low Butte but you didn't show up.'

'Put that down to Cherokee George. He don't like spending time in towns.'

'How did you locate me in the first place?'

'That was easy. I have contacts on the railroad. It only took a bit of asking around to come up with your name. The rest was down to Cherokee George.'

'We knew for sure you were our man when you made for the desert. Not many people would have chosen that option. It was real clever of you to find that water.'

McCleod looked over at Cherokee George. It would have been nothing to him.

'You put me way off course. I was headed for Marmot Wallow till you boys changed the agenda. I need time to think this over,' he said.

'That's fine. We ain't goin' nowhere.'

'One thing I'll need before I make a decision.'

Fogle looked at him.

'What's that?' he said.

'I want my rifle and my six-guns.'

Fogle stared even harder and then his mean face broke into a smile.

'Roy, give him back his guns.'

For just a moment the other man hesitated but then he got to his feet and picked up the Winchester and the gunbelt.

'There you are,' he said.

McCleod fastened the gunbelt round his waist and hefted the rifle.

'OK,' he said. 'I've decided. I'm willin' to ride with you boys but on my own terms.'

'And they are?'

'That I'm under no orders and no obligations. I do as I think fit.'

'Suits us fine,' Fogle said.

McCleod nodded.

'I still got some business in Marmot Wallow,' he said. 'Meet me there in five days' time. I gather Cherokee George ain't partial to towns but he'll have to make an exception. I'll be stayin' at a place called the Occidental. That suit you?'

Fogle looked at Bunce.

'Sure,' he replied. There was some hesitancy about his manner which McCleod couldn't help noticing.

'Don't worry. I'll be there. Now maybe you can fill me in with a few more details.'

The day was still relatively young but they didn't immediately move away from the mesa. McCleod recovered his horse from where he had left it. As he led it towards where the group had agreed to make camp, he met Cherokee George coming in the opposite direction. Cherokee George hadn't said very much earlier. McCleod had a sudden inspiration to try and catch him off guard.

'What's your interest in this?' he said.

Cherokee George's face was impassive.

'Like the man said, I'm gettin' well paid.'

McCleod rubbed his stubbled chin.

'You're goin' to an awful lot of trouble. Now, I could

imagine someone like you might go to some lengths at the prospect of a whole lot of money, but not for what you'd be likely to make from a caper like this.'

'Ain't you forgettin' about the girl?'

McCleod laughed.

'Yeah,' he replied, 'I should have realized the milk of lovin' kindness was just oozin' out of every one of your pores. I guess you care for old lame dogs too; visit your aged mother right there in her little cottage, the one you built for her with your own hands.'

'Regular,' Cherokee George replied.

He grinned, revealing filed down teeth that made him look like a wolf. McCleod pushed his way past. There was little chance of disturbing Cherokee George's equilibrium. The man was inscrutable. Cherokee George stood and watched him as he made his way down the trail before continuing his own way to the top of the mesa.

Late that night McCleod rode out from the mesa, having decided to make ground during the cool of the night. For a while he could see the camp-fire glowing where he had left his three pursuers behind him. He didn't really have any business in Marmot Wallow. He wanted to get away from them and give himself time to think about things. There was something about the situation which didn't quite add up. They had taken a lot of pains to track him down. Was the whole story some kind of sham? The letter from Sandy to him seemed genuine enough. Had Bunce really suspected him of having been involved? And did his addition to the rescue party really make much difference? For the time being he would go along with them. Maybe things would soon become clearer. He had nothing better to do. He had finished his work for the railroad company. He had money in his pocket and no definite plans. In the short term, one thing was as good as another.

He began to recollect the time he had spent on the Kruger spread. Sandy was no real relation to Kruger. Fogle had referred to Sandy as Kruger's daughter, but she wasn't. Some said she had been adopted by Kruger in a vague sort of way after her parents had died in the aftermath of the Civil War. A more likely story was that she was connected through Kruger's woman. Now that he thought about it, maybe Sandy had shown signs of being disaffected even then. She had certainly been self-contained, even a lonely girl. For some reason she had opened up to him, but it wasn't something she'd be likely to make a habit of. So did it make sense that she had become friendly enough with Bunce in a very short space of time, even to the extent of being considered his girlfriend? One thing was certainly odd. For Sandy Kruger to run away once might be explicable, but for her to have done so twice was stretching belief. What was she running away from the second time, when she had disappeared from Cobb Corner? McCleod suddenly jerked in the saddle. Could she have been running from Bunce, or even got word that Fogle was on his way? Could she have known Fogle? Or was she running from Kruger? The questions were racing around in McCleod's head. And he was still trying to figure out the enigmatic Cherokee George.

CHAPTER TWO

McCleod rode into Marmot Wallow early in the morning, stabled his horse at the livery and registered at the Occidental Hotel. Then he made his way to the barber shop, had a bath, haircut and shave and changed into some fresh gear he bought at Thompson and Smith's Clothing Store. Having seen to his basic needs and feeling a different man, he entered the nearest eating house and ordered himself a full fried breakfast with extras and a big pot of black coffee. When he had finished he sat back and regarded the world through the window. The town was coming to life. The boardwalks were filling with people, wagons and buggies rolled down the street and an occasional horseman rode by. Situated on the edge of the canyon country, the place was thriving and there was one particular reason for it: gold. It had been found in the hills west of the badlands. Even as he watched he could see grizzled old men and eager young faces which could only belong to new prospectors making their way to the diggings.

He might have been tempted to try his hand himself except he had done it in the past without reward.

Suddenly he flinched. Coming down the street was Cherokee George! There could be no mistaking the lean figure and measured gait, the high cheekbones and flat features. He was wearing a distinctive wide-brimmed, low-crowned hat with a feather in the side. How could he have got to Marmot Wallow ahead of McCleod? Only by riding flat out and barely stopping for rest. It was obvious from his manner that he was already settled. There had been no sign of his horse at the livery stable. That could easily be accounted for, because there was more than one in town. In any case, McCleod had not been looking out for Cherokee George's paint. Were Fogle and Bunce with him? He watched as Cherokee George carried on walking. When he crossed the sun-drenched dusty drag, McCleod realized he was heading for the eating house. In a moment the bell over the door tinkled and Cherokee George entered. He glanced about quickly and then, without registering the faintest surprise at seeing McCleod there, made for his table. He pulled out a chair and sat down. McCleod had to make an effort not to show his surprise.

'Coffee?' he said.

'It's OK. I'll order some fresh,' Cherokee George replied.

He signalled to the middle-aged waitress and she appeared quickly carrying a pot of coffee and some biscuits. Cherokee George poured out a cup for himself, refilled McCleod's cup and offered him a biscuit. They ate and drank in silence for a few minutes till McCleod could no longer conceal his curiosity.

'What the hell are you doin' in Marmot Wallow?' he said.

Cherokee George looked at him through vacant eyes.

'That was the arrangement,' he said.

McCleod took a drink.

'Are Fogle and Bunce with you?' he asked.

'Nope. But they'll be here soon enough.'

'It ain't five days,' McCleod said.

'They'll be here in a few days. I figured I'd come on ahead.'

'Was that their idea?'

'They didn't object.'

McCleod was at a loss what to make of it.

'I don't like people crowdin' me,' he said.

'I won't get in your way.'

'Where are you stayin'? The Occidental?'

'Folks ain't always too friendly towards what they call a half breed,' Cherokee replied. 'Nope, I ain't stayin' at the Occidental or anywhere else in town. I make my own arrangements.'

McCleod got to his feet.

'Keep outa my way,' he said.

Cherokee George shrugged but did not say anything. McCleod strode to the counter and paid his bill. Opening the door, he stepped out into the sunlight.

A couple of days passed. The next day was the one scheduled for McCleod to meet with Fogle and Bunce. During the course of that time he had only twice seen Cherokee George, making his way through the batwings of the Lucky Strike Saloon. McCleod had been in the saloon once. It was frequented by prospectors either on their way to the diggings or coming back. If they had any money in their pockets, there were plenty of ways for them to lose it. McCleod himself had barely resisted the wiles of the soiled doves on offer and that was mainly because his thoughts were on Sandy Kruger. What if she had ended up in a place like the Lucky Strike and was even now offering her charms to the highest bidder? He remembered her as he had known her at the Cinch Buckle and he didn't like the contrast. He realized then that whatever he had thought about the situation so far, he was now irrevocably committed to finding Sandy Kruger. Apart from that knowledge, he was no nearer arriving at a solution as to what to do next, but he had grown very familiar with Sandy's letter. Two things stood out for him. She had been prepared to leave her horse, Concho, behind. That must have been quite a wrench. Whatever had caused her to leave the ranch, it must have been something pretty important. And perhaps there was a clue to her whereabouts in her notebooks, even her poems. He didn't know enough about such things to have a view, one way or the other.

As he approached the Lucky Strike, the batwings

suddenly flew open and a man crashed to the earth. In a second he was on his feet. It was Cherokee George and even as McCleod recognized him, he was set upon by a group of four men who came hurtling out of the saloon in pursuit. Cherokee swung his arm and one of his attackers went down but he was swept aside by the onslaught and went bowling over. Two of the men flung themselves on top of him while the third swung his boot and brought it crashing into Cherokee's ribs. McCleod didn't wait any longer. In a second he had joined the fray, seizing the leg of Cherokee's attacker as he swung it back for another kick. Down they both went but McCleod landed on top; his fist slammed into the man's face and he ceased to struggle. At the same moment McCleod felt himself being dragged to his feet by two more attackers and while they pinned his arms to his side, another man dug his elbow into his midriff. McCleod gasped and bent over with the shock and pain but he was being held firmly by the other two. Another blow landed in his solar plexus, followed by an uppercut to the chin. He was fighting to stay conscious, waiting for the next blow, when Cherokee, having escaped the attentions of his assailants for a moment, flung himself upon them so that they all went crashing to the ground once more. McCleod's face scraped along the dust and dirt. As he strove to rise, somebody landed on him but he was able to arch his back and the man went flying over his head. His back smashed against a stanchion and he lay inert. McCleod turned his head to see Cherokee's fist send another man to the ground. Dust hung in the air and a crowd had gathered. More men had charged out of the Lucky Strike to join in the attack and the situation didn't look good. Suddenly McCleod's eyes caught a glint of steel and he involuntarily flinched as a Bowie knife descended towards his chest. It never reached its target; Cherokee George's arm shot out, seizing the man's wrist. For a few moments the issue hung in the balance. Their two arms shook with the intensity of the struggle and then the man's hand bent back. There was a sharp crack and he screamed as the knife dropped. McCleod and Cherokee found themselves back to back still facing a menacing crowd when there was the sound of a shot being fired into the air and the crowd parted to allow the entry of the town marshal.

'OK boys, break it up!' he shouted.

A few of the men made to renew the attack but the marshal seized one of them by the shoulder and waved his gun in the man's face.

'I said break it up,' he hissed, 'and I mean it.'

The man hesitated and then spat into the dust.

'OK boys,' he said to the others. 'I guess we taught this no-good Injun varmint a lesson he ain't gonna forget.'

The rest of the men stood for a moment longer, hurling looks of hatred at McCleod and more especially at Cherokee. Then, dusting down their clothes, they made their way back through the batwings into the saloon.

'Ain't you gonna arrest anyone?' McCleod gasped.

The marshal looked him up and down.

'You're lucky it didn't turn to gunplay,' he said. 'As it is, nobody's been killed.'

He bent down to examine the two unconscious men and then turned to some of the bystanders.

'Help me haul these out of the way,' he said.

In a few moments the men had been carried inside the saloon. The marshal reappeared.

'I suggest you two make yourselves scarce,' he said. He gave Cherokee a long hard look and then began to walk away in the direction of his office. Cherokee and McCleod exchanged glances.

'You OK?' Cherokee said.

'Yeah, least I will be. Reckon we're both gonna feel real sore for a whiles.'

McCleod couldn't be sure, but he thought he saw the shred of a grin on Cherokee George's face.

'What was it all about?' he asked.

'You heard what the man called me.'

'This sort of thing happened before?'

Cherokee shrugged.

'I'm part Anglo, part Sioux, part Cherokee. I got Mexican blood too. Seems like it just ain't a popular mix.'

McCleod looked up and down. Things had gone back to normal. Nobody appeared to take any further interest in the two battered figures standing in the middle of the street.

'Come on,' McCleod said. 'I got a bottle of good whiskey in my hotel room.'

'They might object to me there too.'

'Let them try anythin',' McCleod said.

They made their way to the Occidental. The clerk gave them a suspicious glance as they passed his desk and made their way up the staircase.

During the rest of the time that remained till the arrival of Fogle and Bunce Cherokee George made himself scarce. McCleod didn't ask too many questions about where he was staying and Cherokee wasn't saying anything. Either he had found an amenable berth somewhere in town or more likely he was making camp outside in the open. From what he had seen of Cherokee, McCleod favoured the latter. McCleod, too, decided that the best policy might be to lie low. He was happy to meet trouble when it presented itself but he didn't see any reason to go out looking for it. Walking down a side street the following afternoon, he thought he caught some ugly glances from a couple of mean-looking *hombres* he passed but nothing came of it. Still, he was on the alert and his hand wasn't too far from his gunbelt. He was a little surprised that the marshal had not seen fit to remove his six-guns. But then the town of Marmot Wallow didn't seem too anxious to advertise itself as the Cranberry Haven of the West.

At the arranged hour McCleod and Cherokee George sat in the dining room of the Occidental. After they had waited for some while, they ordered lunch. By the time they had finished the last bite of apple pie it was obvious that Fogle and Bunce weren't going to show up.

'Now, I wonder what could have happened to delay them?' McCleod said.

Cherokee George drew his hand across his mouth in lieu of a napkin.

'Can't think of anythin'. They were plumb keen to be on the trail of Miss Kruger.'

'They had plenty of time to get here,' McCleod replied. 'I was half expectin' 'em earlier.'

He poured coffee for himself and Cherokee George and passed his pouch of Bull Durham. They drank, smoked and relaxed. By the time they had finished, the dining room was empty.

'I don't know about you,' Cherokee George said, 'but I reckon I've had enough of this town.'

McCleod looked out of the window one more time.

'Yeah, me also,' he said. 'Let's go and see if we can find those two.'

They got to their feet and walked to the desk where McCleod paid for the meal and his bill. Then they made their way to the livery stables. They looked about for Fogle and Bunce's horses but they weren't there. They led their horses down the runway, mounted and rode out of town.

After being cooped up in Marmot Wallow, both of them felt good to be back in the saddle. They kept riding till the sun was low when Cherokee George pointed to the sky. High in the sun-washed blue some buzzards were circling. They rode on and then Cherokee spotted something in the distance. They drew to a halt and McCleod got out his field glasses.

'A couple of bodies,' he said.

He handed the glasses to Cherokee.

'Reckon we found Fogle and Bunce,' he said.

They spurred their horses. As they approached the bodies the buzzards flapped up into the air like question marks. They dropped from the saddle and approached the corpses. From the moment they had seen the birds there had been no question in their minds of finding anyone alive. Crouching down, they could see that both men had been shot a number of times. McCleod looked about him. There were outcrops of rock and boulders where bushwhackers might have been concealed. Cherokee George examined the ground closely. The earth was hard but he detected traces of hoofs.

'I'd say there were four of them,' he concluded.

He began to walk towards a patch of brush.

'Be careful!' McCleod called.

'There is no one here now,' Cherokee retorted.

He peered about and then returned to where McCleod was standing.

'They went off in that direction,' he said, pointing ahead, in the direction they had been following.

'Maybe we'll pick up some sign further on,' McCleod replied.

He exchanged glances with Cherokee George.

'I guess there ain't nothin' much we can do except bury 'em.'

By the time they had finished that task, night had fallen. McCleod was for setting up camp but Cherokee George disagreed.

'Better to go on,' he said. 'Find some place with water.'

'We got water.'

Cherokee did not reply. Instead he swung into the saddle and began to ride away. Seeing there was no alternative, McCleod climbed into leather and rode after him. They kept on riding in silence. Clouds had gathered and the night was dark. Eventually Cherokee drew to a halt. Off to their right a few drooping willows indicated the presence of a stream.

'Over there,' Cherokee said. 'It is a good place.'

Cherokee was right. It was a better place than the one McCleod had chosen. Still, McCleod was a little puzzled by Cherokee's behaviour. They soon had a fire going. McCleod laid slabs of bacon in the pan. It was a long time since they had eaten and he was hungry. It tasted fine. Afterwards they lay back drinking thick black coffee. They built smokes. The gathering wind moaned in the drooping leaves and the stream purled. Cherokee George turned to his companion.

'I never said thanks for helpin' me out back there in town,' he said.

McCleod was surprised. He hadn't figured Cherokee George to be the type to express his feelings. Suddenly he thought he knew why Cherokee hadn't wanted to stay and make camp near where they had buried Fogle and Bunce. Maybe it was the Indian blood in him.

'Still feel sore,' he said, 'but it was worth it.'

They relapsed into silence again. McCleod finished his cigarette and built another. He passed his pouch of tobacco to Cherokee George.

'Those two bein' killed puts a different slant on things,' he said.

Cherokee George lit his tightly rolled smoke.

'Yeah,' he said. 'I guess it does.'

'So who do you reckon was responsible?'

Cherokee George shook his head.

'Maybe their killings had nothin' to do with this business of Miss Sandy Kruger's disappearance. But it don't seem likely,' McCleod continued.

'There was no sign of their horses. Whoever done it, took their horses.'

'Yeah, and whoever it was, they're out there somewhere. Somewhere close. And if there is a connection to Miss Sandy, they'll be lookin' for us next.'

They both stared out beyond the closed circle of dancing flames. Beyond the reaches of the firelight, the darkness seemed to crouch like an animal.

'I reckon the time's come for you to come clean,' McCleod said.

He avoided looking in Cherokee's direction. There was no response from him. McCleod waited a minute or two longer.

'Was it you killed Fogle and Bunce?' he said.

Cherokee drew deeply on his cigarette. It seemed he was going to remain silent and McCleod was almost taken by surprise when after a long gap he finally spoke.

'I can see how it might look that way, but it weren't me.'

'Who was it then? I figure you know a lot more

than you're sayin'.'

Again there was no immediate response from Cherokee.

'Durin' the time I was kickin' my heels in Marmot Wallow,' McCLeod continued, 'I got to doin' some thinkin'. So let me just throw a little somethin' into the meltin' pot to start you goin'. Fogle was more than a bit vague about his role in all this. One thing I reckon for sure is that he was never a member of the Texas Rangers. I figure it's more likely he was wanted by the Texas Rangers.'

'You're wrong,' Cherokee replied. 'Fogle was a Texas Ranger. He left because word got put around that he was in with some of the outlaws he was supposed to be after. There weren't no truth in it, but he was under a cloud. Later on he thought he'd found out who it was that spread the rumours. It was somebody whose trail he had been on for some time for cattle rustlin' across the Rio Bravo. That man was Kruger.'

'Go on,' McCleod said.

'Kruger led a gang of bandits. They also operated on the Brazos and other rivers that had to be crossed by trail herds following the trails north from San Antonio. A lot of cattle got run off. It was easy pickin's. I guess that's where Kruger got the money to buy himself the Hog Eye and set himself up as a respectable rancher.'

'How do you know this?'

'I rode with Kruger's bandits for a time. I was one of them. It was then I first heard about Fogle. He was on to Kruger. Kruger realized it. He got out before Fogle got a chance to bring him in.'

'What happened to the gang?'

'The gang split up. People went their separate ways, some of 'em straight into the penitentiary. I'd seen the light before then. It was a mug's game. Kruger was the only one to benefit. He ended up with the Hog Eye and smellin' of roses.'

'I still don't quite see where this is goin'.'

'When Kruger got out with all the loot and bought up the Hog Eye, that wasn't all he took. He also took Fogle's woman.'

'I'm beginnin' to see the picture,' McCleod said.

'You ain't seen it all. There's more. Fogle's woman had a sister. She went along too. That sister is Miss Sandy.'

'How do you know all this?'

'It ain't hard. I keep my ear to the ground. A lot of this was common knowledge. Later on, I did some odd jobs around the Cinch Buckle. That's Kruger's latest spread. I don't know whether Kruger remembered me at all from the days he was rustlin' cattle. I doubt it. I was a very small cog in his machine.'

'So what happened to bring all this to a head?'

'You mean Miss Sandy runnin' away? This is where I ain't so sure of my facts. That's partly why I'm here. Piecin' things together, I figure it's this way. Like I said, Fogle was disgraced. His woman left him. For a long time he just dropped out of the picture. I heard he was in a bad way, gettin' by as a saddle tramp and hittin' the whiskey bottle. Some folks I know in

Abilene told me he was livin' as a hobo in a jungle camp outside of town. Somehow or other, he must have pieced himself together again.'

'So he came back on the scene.'

'I reckon that as Miss Sandy got older, she got to hear rumours. She was always somethin' of an outcast. Kruger didn't have much use for her. When Fogle's ex-woman died, she was way out on a limb. The way I see it is, she could have run off at any time, but somethin' happened to trigger her into finally doin' it. Fogle got to hear of it. He decided to set out to try to find her.'

'Because she was his wife's sister? She must have been pretty young when she went to live with Kruger.'

'I figure he'd lost interest in Kruger. He didn't have enough originally to nail him. He might not have even been aware that Kruger was behind his fall from grace.'

McCleod was thinking hard.

'Maybe Miss Sandy's disappearance did have an effect on him. Maybe the fact that she was family really meant somethin'.'

He looked at Cherokee George.

'What about Bunce?' he said.

'Bunce is exactly what he said he was. He met Miss Sandy in Cobb Corner and struck up a friendship with her. That part of the story is simple. He volunteered to come with us to find her.'

'And my involvement? Is that the way you told it?'

'Yeah. Finding that letter was the crucial thing.

Bunce seemed to set a lot of store by gettin' you involved in the search. Once Fogle traced you to the railroad company, it was easy enough for me to lead them to you.'

McCleod looked out into the darkness again.

'That kinda brings us back to where we started this conversation,' he said. 'Who killed Fogle and Bunce? And what are they likely to be plannin' next?'

He thought hard.

'It's got to be someone who wanted to stop Fogle and Bunce from finding Miss Sandy. Fogle in particular. And the only person I can figure who might have an interest in that is Kruger. What's more, from what you've told me, he had his own reasons for not wanting Fogle around. It must have come as a bit of a shock to him to find his old enemy back on the scene again.'

Cherokee George had been listening intently but if McCleod expected a response he was disappointed. Instead he muttered something and then held up his hand.

'Listen!' he hissed.

McCleod paused and strained his ears, but he could hear nothing.

'Riders,' Cherokee said.

'I can't hear anythin'. They must be a good ways off.'

'Yeah, but they're comin' this way. From somewhere up ahead of us.'

They got to their feet and poured the remains of the coffee over the dwindling flames of the camp-fire.

'Do you figure they've seen anythin'?' McCleod said.

Cherokee shook his head.

'The place is well concealed. That's why I chose it.'

'Then we'll stay right here and if they come by this way, they'll find a welcomin' committee just waitin' for 'em.'

Quickly, they moved their horses further into the shelter of the willow trees. As they did so, McCleod reflected that maybe he had been wrong about Cherokee George's motives. Perhaps he had simply chosen the campsite for the reason he had stated – that it was well concealed. Maybe it had had nothing to do with Fogle and Bunce – what was left of them. When they were satisfied that they had left no apparent traces of their presence, they checked their guns and waited.

It seemed to McCleod that they had been waiting a long time before he even heard the riders. Then very gradually the steady drumming of their horses' hoofs drew closer.

'There's quite a bunch of 'em,' Cherokee whispered. 'I reckon if it's the same ones killed Fogle and Bunce, they been joined by some others.'

The noise of the approaching horses was loud now and Cherokee George's keen eyes were the first to see them. They were riding in a tight bunch but he felt pretty sure there were eight of them. McCleod, too, could now see them. They grew steadily nearer and then suddenly the drumming of the hoofs ceased. The night felt strangely quiet.

'What are they doin'?' McCleod said.

'I think they're suspicious about somethin'.'

'Maybe they saw our fire after all.'

'Nope. I figure their horses picked up the scent of ours.'

The riders began to move forward again, approaching slowly. McCleod raised his Winchester. Cherokee George's finger tightened round the trigger of his .50 Sharps. Suddenly the night was illuminated by a jet of flame and a bullet tore into the trees behind which they were crouched. In another instant the darkness erupted in a blaze of fire and a thunder of shooting. Slugs tore into the trees, bringing down some branches and sending cascades of shards and splinters flying into the air. McCleod and Cherokee opened fire at the same time, aiming at the flashes of light that betrayed the whereabouts of their attackers. Horses began to scream and some of them reared, unshipping their riders. Other riders slid from the saddle to take whatever shelter they could find or else lie prone on the ground. McCleod and Cherokee had had time to mark their targets and they both sensed that their fire had been effective. Bullets were still singing all around them but the intensity of the fire rapidly lessened. They could hear men shouting to each other and dim shapes running away into the night. Through the gloom they could see a couple of riders who were still in the saddle help two of their comrades climb up behind them and then, with a final volley, the ones who remained galloped off into the surrounding darkness.

McCleod fired a last shot and then turned to Cherokee George.

'I think they've had enough,' he said.

'Yeah, for now,' Cherokee said.

They waited in case their assailants decided to return to the attack, but the sounds of horses had vanished. The only noise they could hear was someone groaning. After a time the groaning stopped and the silence seemed even more palpable. The eastward sky was beginning to lighten when Cherokee got to his feet, followed by McCleod. Cautiously, they moved forward, leaving the shelter of the trees. Three of their attackers lay inert, together with two of the horses. Getting close, they could see that all were dead. McCleod turned to Cherokee.

'Recognize any of these?' he asked.

Cherokee George nodded.

'I recognize two of 'em,' he said. 'They used to work at the Cinch Buckle.'

McCleod grunted.

'Then I was right,' he said. 'Looks like Kruger is behind this. It must have been Kruger who killed Fogle and Bunce.'

'One thing's for sure,' Cherokee George replied. 'Whether it's Kruger or somebody else, they ain't gonna let this go. They'll be lookin' for revenge.'

'Yeah, and I reckon there'll be a lot more of 'em, especially when Kruger gets to know what's happened. He'll be sure to call up reinforcements. I reckon we can expect a pretty hot time of it.'

'I don't expect they'll make the same mistakes they made tonight,' Cherokee said. 'They'll learn from what happened here.'

Bright waves of dawn were breaking over the landscape. Quickly, McCleod and Cherokee George saddled up the horses.

'Sure could do with somethin' to eat,' Cherokee George said.

McCleod cut them both a few strips of jerky.

'No time to hang around,' he said. 'We can think about breakfast later. Right now we need to get ridin' and put distance between ourselves and this place.'

Cherokee George finished fastening the girths on his pinto.

'I got no quarrel with that,' he said. 'But just where in hell are we aimin' for?'

'For Cobb Corner,' McCleod replied.

'Cobb Corner?'

'That was the last place anyone saw Miss Sandy,' McCleod replied.

A thin smile raised the edges of Cherokee's lips, exposing his filed-down teeth.

'It's a long ride,' he said. 'Reckon we'd best get started.'

CHAPTER THREE

Nobody knew the full name of Kruger, the owner of the Cinch Buckle. To all who were acquainted with him he was simply known as W.D. On this particular evening he was not in a good mood, despite having just eaten an excellent meal in the dining room of the Rectifying Hotel in Cobb Corner. He had taken a couple of their best rooms, joined by an interconnecting doorway, and now sat on a balcony high above the main street of town. In his hand was a glass of the best rye and in his mouth a fine cigar but neither seemed to improve his attitude. He had traced his wife's sister this far, but he had arrived only to find her gone. As if that wasn't bad enough, he had learned that he wasn't the only one looking for her, and from what information he had been able to garner, it appeared that the person involved was none other than his old enemy, Carl Fogle. He had dispatched some of his men to try and locate Fogle with orders to kill him and whoever else might be riding with him. He figured he had dealt too lightly with Fogle in the past; this time he didn't intend making any such mistake. But he was peeved that there should be any necessity for the whole state of affairs to have arisen. Who was Sandra anyway to have spurned his advances? A chit of a girl he had taken in and provided for all this time. Where would she have been when her sister died, without his protection and the shelter he had been kind enough to provide? Hell, she owed him! He felt a prick of desire at the recollection of her lithe thin body and wide eyes. But that was only part of the story. Much more important than anything was that box she had taken to keep her notebooks in, those notebooks filled with her stupid poems. Really, none of the rest mattered. But that box sure did. In fact, it was all important.

Night had fallen and the main street of Cobb Corner was quiet. Light spilled from the batwing doors of the Tin Cup Saloon but there wasn't much happening. A number of horses were fastened to the hitch rail, among them a few bearing the Cinch Buckle brand. Presently the batwings swung aside and the figure of Jepson, Kruger's foreman, appeared. He stepped down from the boardwalk and began to walk rapidly towards the hotel. Kruger tossed off the rest of his whiskey and went indoors. Something about Jepson's walk looked purposeful. He hadn't long to wait till there was a knock on the door.

'Come in!' Kruger called.

The door opened and Jepson stepped into the room.

'Hope I ain't disturbin' you, boss,' he said.

'Of course not. Take a seat. I figure you wouldn't say no to a glass of whiskey? It's good stuff.'

He poured the whiskey and offered Jepson a cigar which he refused.

'I think we might be on to somethin',' Jepson said.

'Yeah? What's that?'

'I got talkin' to a fella in the saloon earlier. He knows somebody helps out over at the stage depot. He reckoned he might have seen a woman answering to the description of Miss Sandy take a morning stage outa town.'

'When was this?'

'He said it must have been about four days ago. He couldn't be sure exactly.'

'It doesn't matter. We could check on that. They should have a record at the depot. Where was the stage headed?'

'Superstition, but there's a lot of stops on the way.'

'Superstition?'

Kruger seemed to dwell on the name for a few moments.

'Well, at least that gives us somethin' to go on,' he concluded. 'You did well.'

'You could maybe have a word with the man yourself. I gather he spends a lot of time at the Tin Cup.'

Kruger looked out towards the saloon.

'I might do that,' he said.

Jepson swallowed the last of his whiskey and made to get to his feet.

'There's no hurry,' Kruger said. 'Stick around for

a while. Here, have another drink.'

Jepson sat down again while Kruger refilled his glass.

'We've spent a lot of time on this already,' Kruger said. 'I don't want to wait around here too long.'

'The rest of the boys should be back soon,' Jepson replied.

Kruger seemed to consider his words.

'What's the first stage halt after Cobb Corner?' he finally asked.

'Gunnison. Not sure what comes after that, though.'

Kruger reflected for a moment.

'I know the place. Ain't nothin' to it. She won't get out there.'

He turned to Jepson.

'Go down to the depot tomorrow morning,' he said. 'Get hold of a list of all the stops between here and Superstition. Maybe we can work out where she would be likely to get off.'

'I could check out where she took a ticket to.'

'You could try. But if she's been spooked into movin' on because she knows we're lookin' for her, she's probably wise to that one. She'd be more likely to try and trick us and get off anywhere.'

Jepson gave Kruger a sharp look but didn't say anything. The way Kruger had spoken, it didn't seem like it was a straightforward runaway situation. It looked like it might be more complicated than that, otherwise why would Miss Sandy resort to tricks? Kruger lit another cigar.

'Sure you don't want one?' he said.

'Sure.'

Jepson stood up.

'I'll get over to the depot first thing. Thanks for the whiskey.'

Kruger opened the door and stood there listening as his foreman's boots shuffled down the carpeted stairs. When he had gone he switched the lamp down low. For a long time he lay on the bed, watching a corner of the sky through the doorway to the balcony, reflecting on what he would do to Miss Sandy once he had found her.

Miss Sandy Kruger hadn't intended to leave Cobb Corner. In fact, she was beginning to like it there. It was pleasant to sit on the veranda in the evenings after a day's work in the store. She had quickly made friends and though Bunce appeared to be more struck on her than she would have liked, it was nice to have someone to talk to. He seemed a pleasant young man. He approached her with respect; such a contrast to how some of the ranch-hands had treated her. And Kruger, of course. She almost shivered when she thought of him. What had happened since her sister's death to make him change? Or had he always been that way? It was horrible and she didn't even want to think about it. The one thing which would have made her new life even better would have been to have her horse, Concho, to ride. She hoped someone would look after it.

Then one day, looking out of the window of the

general store, she had seen someone she thought was from the Cinch Buckle. The store was quiet and she had watched as he walked down the street. Her heart had skipped a beat when it seemed he might come into the shop but he had walked straight on past. She had watched him till he rounded a corner. She was shaking. What was someone from the Cinch Buckle doing in Cobb Corner? It could only mean that Kruger had decided to follow her. That was something she hadn't reckoned on. Was he here, in Cobb Corner, already? Or had he sent his man ahead of him to investigate? She was confused and frightened. It seemed the only thing to do was to get away from Cobb Corner fast.

The stagecoach rattled along. There were a number of other passengers. When they had boarded the stage she had examined them anxiously, half expecting the Cinch Buckle man to be amongst them. Now she was beginning to feel a little more relaxed. How far was it to Low Butte? She began to speculate. Maybe it hadn't been any of Kruger's riders she had seen. She hadn't got that good a sight of him. One cowboy resembled another. She started to wonder whether she had done the right thing. Maybe she had been too precipitate. Well, it was too late now. Maybe at some time in the future, when things had blown over, she might return to Cobb Corner. The more she thought about it, however, the more incomprehensible Kruger's behaviour began to appear. He had made perfectly clear to her what his intentions were. She shuddered when she thought of his lascivious talk, the touch of his fingers on her knee, the time he had tried to take her in his arms; all those things ending in that last night when she had had to barricade herself in her room to keep him away from her. It was perfectly clear to her that she had had to get away from the Cinch Buckle, but it was far from clear why Kruger should want to carry on his pursuit of her. Then she started thinking again that maybe the man she had seen in Cobb Corner was nothing to do with Kruger and the Cinch Buckle. Her head was in a spin. Perhaps she was being foolish, acting in a childish manner rather than in the manner of the young woman she felt herself to be.

She became aware that the stage was slowing down; looking out of the window she saw they were arriving at a way-station. The stagecoach drew up in the dusty yard and the driver leaned out.

'We break for half an hour. Get out and stretch your legs.'

One of the passengers opened the door and helped her down. The rest of the passengers made their way into the low wooden building where a pot of coffee was bubbling on the stove. Miss Sandy found a bench outside and sat down. She drew a pencil from her bag and opened a pocket-sized note-book. After thinking for a moment or two, she began to write. Her brows knitted with concentration, she was lost to the world around her. Only when she heard the voice of the driver shouting that it was time to leave did she emerge from her reverie. She glanced at what she had written.

In the deep woods an old gnarled tree,
Leaning, seems to sleep and dream.
Scarred its bark and mossy now,
Grey sky tangled in its boughs.
The wind among those branches shakes
The listless leaves. The tree awakes:

The driver was mounting to his seat. She would have to leave the poem unfinished. The imagery of the poem was a far cry from her surroundings and from her situation, both of which now jerked her back to reality. Replacing the pencil and notebook, she made her way over to the stagecoach and stepped inside. The driver's whip cracked. The wheels raised clouds of dust and the stage lurched forward. She found she was thinking of Concho.

It was soon apparent to Cherokee George that he and McCleod were being followed. Not only that, but there were other riders ahead of them going the same way.

'They came from that direction,' he said. 'Looks like some of 'em at least are goin' back where they come from.'

They drew rein. McCleod's brows were knitted in thought.

'We know they're some of Kruger's men,' he said. 'Seems to me maybe Fogle wasn't the only one to trace Miss Sandy to Cobb Corner.'

'You're figurin' somethin'?' Cherokee replied.

'Maybe Miss Sandy left Cobb Corner because she knew they were comin'. We were goin' to go there to try and find some clue about where she might have gone. What's the best way to get out of Cobb Corner, maybe the only way for a person in her situation?'

'I don't know. You tell me.'

'The stage line. The railroad ain't reached there yet. She might have taken a horse or a horse and buggy, but that don't seem likely. As far as I know, the stage from Low Butte runs through Cobb Corner all the way to Superstition.'

'How do you know that?'

McCleod grinned.

'Remember, I waited in Low Butte for you *hombres* to appear. I had to put in the time somehow.'

Suddenly he clicked his fingers.

'That's it!' he said. 'Low Butte.'

'What are you talkin' about? Low Butte?'

'Listen. Where would you expect Miss Sandy to go if she got on the stage?'

'As far as possible, I guess. Like you say, Superstition is the end of the line.'

'Yeah, and that's exactly what Kruger would reckon. But what if Miss Sandy is cleverer than that? What if she went in the other direction, even if it was takin' her back towards the Cinch Buckle?'

'You mean to Low Butte?'

'Yeah.'

'So what are you sayin''?'

McCleod shook his head.

'You might be real good when it comes to trackin', but you ain't worth a bean when it comes to other things.'

Cherokee George's expression was unreadable.

'This is what I'm thinkin',' McCleod continued. 'We give Cobb Corner a miss. Instead, we follow that stage route; see if we can pick up any sign of Miss Sandy at Low Butte. If we do that, we'll have the added advantage of giving our friends behind us the slip. If I'm right about this, the whole bunch of 'em will end up in Cobb Corner, but we'll be ahead of 'em. Even if Miss Sandy ain't in Low Butte, we won't lose much time. In that case, we just turn right around and aim for Superstition.'

'That's an awful lot of speculatin',' Cherokee George replied. 'But I figure you've got to be right about that stagecoach.'

'OK. Now it's up to you. You tell me which way we ought to go to shake off these varmints and cut across the stage line as quick as possible.'

Cherokee glanced around.

'That stream we camped at,' he said, 'leads to a river. We ride there.'

'Where's that?'

'In the wrong direction to start with, but once we've confused Kruger's boys, we double back.'

'You're the boss,' McCleod said.

Touching their spurs to their horses' flanks, they turned in a different direction.

It took them an hour and a half to reach the river. Coming through a fringe of cottonwoods and willow, they splashed into the water. It was shallow, at no point reaching as high as the horses' knees. As they rode, Cherokee George took pains to brush an over-hanging twig or bend a leaf. After a time they rode out of the water on the opposite side, leaving marks in the muddy banks. They rode up into the trees on that side and then Cherokee George signalled for them both to dismount. Tearing off strips of material from a shirt, he covered the horses' feet. Then they rode along the opposite bank before dropping down to the river again. Cherokee removed the rags and they retraced their steps, going past their initial point of entry and carrying on upstream.

'Wouldn't fool no Indian,' Cherokee George grinned, 'but it should be enough to fool a few *gringos.*'

They continued riding till the river began to widen, at which point they turned off, leaving the river behind them. They were in open, rolling country with stands of trees and shallow dips. It was good country for riding and they set about putting distance between themselves and their pursuers. Towards evening clouds rolled in from the west, presaging a storm. Thunder began to rumble and occasional streaks of lightning flickered along the horizon. Satisfied that they had left their pursuers behind, they made camp before the storm broke.

All the rest of the way to Low Butte Miss Sandy's thoughts were occupied with Concho, the horse she had left behind. It was part mustang and, although used to the rope, had never been ridden before. McCleod had broken him in and she remembered the gentle way he had talked to the horse while getting it used to having a saddle on its back. It was as though the man's assurance and calmness had been transmitted to the horse. When he had finally stepped into the saddle, the mustang had bucked and pitched, but he seemed able to anticipate its movements. No matter what the horse attempted, he had clung on. When he had finished and the horse had been led back to the stable, he had suggested she rub it down with a handful of hay before feeding and watering it. When the time was right, she watched while he shoed it, explaining to her what he was doing and why. Then, when the horse was ready for her to ride, he had given her a special full-stamped saddle made from prime leather. He had never said where he had got it from. She felt like crying when she recalled how beautiful it was. And then, thinking of the saddle, she knew that she would not stay in Low Butte. Instead, she would make her way somehow to the Cinch Buckle and rescue her horse. Re-united with Concho, she would ride somewhere far away where Kruger would have no chance of ever finding her.

The stage began to slow and then, as the first outlying structures began to appear, rolled steadily into Low Butte. There was a small crowd of people hanging about the depot and she felt slightly apprehensive but her common sense told her that there was no way she could have been discovered so quickly. Alighting from the stage, she began to make her way down the street towards the hotel. It was getting late. She decided she would stay overnight, work out what would be the best way to make her way back to the Cinch Buckle, and start afresh the next morning. As she walked down the street she kept darting her gaze from side to side, looking about her, feeling conspicuous. The town was bigger than she had expected and her route took her past a number of shops and stores which were busy with customers. One of them was Hart's Clothing Store and she was about to pass when she had a sudden inspiration. Stopping in her tracks, she turned and walked back. As she entered the store a bell chimed behind her, summoning a middle-aged man with sleeked-back hair. At his presence she suddenly felt awkward.

'Good afternoon, madame. How can I be of help?'

She glanced about. The store was well stocked with men's clothing.

'I am looking for some things for my cousin,' she said.

'Your cousin?'

'Yes. He's visiting, spending a few days in town. He's from back east. I have a feeling he may not bring appropriate things to wear with him.'

The storeman looked at her steadily. He did not recall seeing her in town before but he was too discreet to say anything.

'Certainly, madame. I think we can deal with any requirements your cousin might be likely to have. What size would he be?'

Sandy felt flustered.

'Oh, about my size, I suppose.'

'I see. And would you have any particular items in mind?'

'Well, I suppose pretty much a full outfit.' She hesitated before turning her eyes on the storeman. 'Perhaps you could advise me?'

When she emerged from the store a quarter of an hour later, she was carrying a number of parcels. She booked in at the hotel and made her way up the carpeted stairs to her room. When she had turned the key in the lock and entered, she heaved a huge sigh of relief and then flung herself upon the bed. She lay for quite a long time before getting to her feet. She checked that the door was locked and the window curtain drawn and then began to undo the parcels, laying out the clothes on the bed. Slowly, she took her own clothes off and started to replace them with the items she had bought. She experienced an odd mixture of feelings – awkwardness, shyness, embarrassment – but when she had completed the transformation she felt a sudden sense of relief. She stood in front of the mirror and examined herself. Somehow, the change did not look convincing, but she could work on it. She particularly liked the Stetson and tried placing it on her head at different angles. She was struck by the incongruousness of the situation and couldn't help breaking into a laugh. She tried walking up and down the room. How did a man walk? For a few moments she felt impelled to change back in to her own clothing, but then decided to give it a little time. Maybe she would get more used to it after a while. At least her hair was short. Turning back to the items she had laid on the bed, she took up her pencil and, opening her notebook to the uncompleted poem, sat for a few moments looking at herself in the mirror. Finally, she wrote down some lines in conclusion:

The rustle of the foliage disturbs,
Like nestling memories, a throng of birds.

The morning after the storm broke fine and clear. The rain-washed sky was a limpid blue and the breeze felt clean on McCleod's face as he rode the Morgan alongside Cherokee's pinto. Although he had confidence in Cherokee, he kept looking about him at the long, rolling prairie. Kruger's men were still somewhere about and they would need to be on the alert. It was a long ride to Low Butte. Being watchful did not prevent him enjoying the ride, though. It was a beautiful day. He felt good. He glanced at his companion's face. His expression gave no indication of his state of mind and McCleod fell to wondering again about Cherokee George's motives. In the end he gave up. Cherokee was a good man to have on your side. Whatever doubts he might have about him, his action in coming to Cherokee's help when he was set upon in Marmot Wallow seemed to have bound them together. Leastways, taking into account what Cherokee had said, it was fair to assume that was the case. Cherokee George didn't say a lot. That he had expressed thanks at McCleod's intervention was significant. Suddenly he felt a wave of confidence run through him. He pulled his horse to a halt and after a moment, Cherokee did likewise.

'What is it?' Cherokee asked.

McCleod turned to him with a thin smile on his face.

'Yesterday,' he said, 'you worked out a way of throwin' Kruger's gun-totin' varmints off our trail. Seems like we sure enough lost 'em.'

'Yeah. We sure did.'

For a moment Cherokee's filed teeth showed.

'How about we find 'em again? Only this time on our terms.'

'I could do that,' Cherokee replied.

'I figure we don't neither of us like bein' put on the back foot,' McCleod said. 'Besides, I reckon we owe it to Fogle and Bunce.'

'Those gunnies already been made to pay back part of what they owe.'

'Yeah, maybe so. How about we make them pay the rest?'

'Thought we were headed for Low Butte?'

'We still are. Let's just call this a little detour.'

Cherokee George, shielding his eyes against the strengthening sun, looked all about him.

'Need the glasses?' McCleod asked.

'No. A bunch of those varmints are off in that direction.'

He indicated with his arm.

'I guess they're the ones still lookin' for us.'

'OK,' McCleod replied. 'Let's go and re-introduce ourselves.'

'I got a better idea,' Cherokee George said.

'Yeah? What's that?'

'We were originally headin' for Cobb Corner. That's where we figure Kruger and his gang are goin' to be meetin' up.'

'Sure, prior to them headin' for Superstition.'

'Then why don't we carry on. If we ride hard, we should get there ahead of his boys, or at least about the same time. If Kruger is in Cobb Corner, we could deal with him before they even arrive.'

McCleod thought it over. The thought had occurred to him.

'Kruger ain't likely to be travellin' light. There'll be a big bunch of 'em even without the arrival of these others. It could get kinda messy.'

Cherokee shrugged.

'Sooner or later we gonna have to face them.'

McCleod was still weighing up the pros and cons. There were so many that it became impossible to weigh them all in the balance. One immediate issue they were presented with was whether they could make it to Cobb Corner in advance of Kruger's gun-slicks who were on their way to join him. If they were going to have any chance, they needed to get moving straight away.

'Hell,' McCleod said, 'You're right. Whether it's here or there we gotta face those varmints, and I figure it might as well be there.'

Cherokee grinned.

'What are we waitin' for?' McCleod concluded. 'Let's ride!'

*

Once she had made her decision about making her way back to the Cinch Buckle, Miss Sandy felt a lot better. The question was: how to get there? Leaving her bags at the hotel reception desk, the next morning she made her way to the stage depot to inquire about stagecoaches that might take her in the direction of the nearest railroad stop which in turn would carry her to Redwing, the closest town to the Cinch Buckle spread. She was wearing her normal attire. A night wasn't enough to accustom herself to her new gear and she didn't feel ready to put her new image to the test. The answer to her query was both good and bad. There was a stage which would take her through to Franklin, from which she could catch a train. However, it didn't leave for three days. Thanking the man at the depot, she began to wander slowly back through the town. She didn't relish the thought of having to wait around in Low Butte. Having made up her mind, she was anxious to put her plan into effect. At the same time, she was nervous of meeting anybody from the Cinch Buckle or even running into Kruger himself. If she stayed in Low Butte, she would need to book in again at the hotel. She needed time to think things through. Coming alongside a sign that read *Dolores' Eating Rooms* she stopped and went inside. The place was quiet. Only one other woman sat at a table near the window. A middle-aged woman with black hair tied back in a bun shuffled from behind the counter.

'Just coffee,' Sandy said.

She glanced across at the other woman and felt a sudden pang somewhere in her chest. She looked comfortable. Maybe she was going on to work behind the counter of one of the stores. Maybe she was visiting town. Maybe she had dropped in during the course of a leisurely stroll. How nice it must be to be her. She suddenly felt the loneliness and insecurity of her own position.

Just then the middle-aged lady from behind the counter, who Sandy reckoned must be Dolores, appeared with a pot of coffee, a cup and a saucer. On the edge of the saucer was a biscuit. It was a little gesture but it brought stinging tears to Sandy's eyes.

'Are you all right, my dear?' the woman asked.

'Yes, thank you.'

The woman withdrew. Sandy dabbed at her eyes with a corner of her handkerchief and then poured a cup of coffee. It was good and after she had taken a few sips she felt better. She glanced out of the window. A buggy was just passing and as she looked at it she decided what she should do. She would hire a wagon and drive it to Franklin. She took another drink and unconsciously began to eat the biscuit. Yes, she would hire a wagon. The thought frightened her a little at first but the more she thought abut it the more she liked it. People had driven wagons all the way to Oregon and California. She could look after herself. And when she changed back into those men's clothes she had bought at the clothing emporium, no one would be able to tell she was not a man.

By the time she had finished and paid for the coffee, she was ready to put her plan into operation. Maybe she would drive all the way to Redwing and the Cinch Buckle, and keep a diary of her travels to make use of later. She could mine it for her poetry. Feeling a lot better, she stepped out into the street. She was just about to cross over when she shrank back into the shelter of the eating house wall. Coming towards her on the opposite side was someone she thought she recognized. Taking care to remain in the shadows, she observed the man. As he came opposite he glanced up and looked towards the eating house. For a moment she thought he must see her but in a moment he resumed walking. She followed him with her eyes until he turned a corner and vanished from sight. She put her hand to her chest and took a deep breath. Although she hadn't seen him for a long time, she was convinced that the person she had seen was Carl Fogle.

CHAPTER FOUR

McCleod and Cherokee George sat their horses in the shelter of some trees and looked down on the ramshackle buildings that constituted the town of Cobb Corner.

'We ain't seen any of Kruger's gunnies on the way here,' McCleod said. 'Are you sure we got here in time?'

Cherokee George shifted the wad of tobacco he was chewing from one side of his mouth to the other.

'I'm sure,' he said. 'They're at least a day behind.'

'Assumin' we're right about all this, Kruger's already in Low Butte with some of his men waitin' for the rest to join him before they all move out. I been thinkin'. Maybe we should wait till the whole bunch of 'em is gathered together before we do anythin'.'

Cherokee was silent for a moment or two, his jaws moving as he chewed the tobacco. Then he turned to McCleod.

'Makes sense,' he said, 'but I got to say I'm gettin' plumb restless for some action.'

McCleod looked closely at Cherokee. There

seemed to be something strained about the man's demeanour, as if he was holding something back, as if some latent energy was beginning to demand release. He realized that he was feeling that way himself. Suddenly he laughed; a wolfish grin raised the corners of Cherokee's mouth.

'Yeah,' he said. 'Me too. I'm about tired of tryin' to work things out. Never mind waitin' any longer. Let's go get 'em!'

Wheeling away, they rode on towards the town. It didn't take long for them to reach the outlying buildings but instead of carrying on down the main street, they turned off and took a back way towards the centre of town. Rather than tie up immediately at one of the hitch rails, they made their way to the livery stables. It seemed to McCleod that the ostler was wary of them. He produced a wad of notes and pressed some into the man's hand.

'Strangers in town?' he asked.

'You mean, apart from you two?'

'Yeah, that's what I mean.'

The ostler gave Cherokee George a suspicious look.

'A bunch of 'em,' the man said. 'Arrived in town not long ago.'

'They been causin' trouble?'

'Not exactly. Some. Guess it just don't feel comfortable havin' them here.'

'Any idea who they are?'

Again the ostler looked uneasily at Cherokee George.

'Let me take a guess,' McCleod said. 'They belong to an outfit called the Cinch Buckle?'

The man hesitated a moment and then nodded.

'Where can we find 'em,' Cherokee interposed.

'That's easy. They spend a lot of time at the Tin Cup.'

'Where's that?' McCleod said.

'Right in the middle of town. You can't miss it.'

McCleod turned to Cherokee and then back to the ostler.

'You ain't heard anythin' of a young woman by the name of Sandy Kruger?' he asked on an off chance.

The man shook his head.

'Give the hosses a good feed,' McCleod said.

When the ostler had tended to the horses, McCleod and Cherokee mounted up and rode out of the livery stable. The sun was high and glaring and beat back from the washed-out clapboard buildings. A bunch of tumbleweed came dancing down the street, blown along by a rising breeze. They came to a corner and turned; the next corner brought them to the main street of town. They glanced up and down. The ostler was right. There was no mistaking the Tin Cup. Even at this hour of day a good number of horses were tied to the hitch rail and as they got closer the tinny notes of a piano reached their ears. They dismounted and tied their horses to the hitching post, stopping for a moment to examine the other horses. A number of them carried the Cinch Buckle brand. They stepped on to the boardwalk and then brushed through the batwing doors. The place was busy; a few people sitting at the tables glanced up at their arrival. Standing at the bar was a group of men that were unmistakably the ones they were looking for. Their attitude and their attire singled them out from most of the other townsfolk. They moved grudgingly aside to make a little more space at the bar.

'What'll it be, gentlemen?' the bartender asked.

'Whiskey.'

The bartender poured the drinks. McCleod and Cherokee put their feet up on the rail. One of the saloon girls made to approach them but at a glance from McCleod she changed her mind and sat down at a nearby table. McCleod threw back the whiskey and then turned to the barman.

'We're lookin' for a man named Kruger,' he said.

The barman shook his head.

'Don't think I know anyone of that name,' he replied.

McCleod was watching the group of men at the bar in the mirror. They hadn't been able to conceal their interest at the mention of Kruger's name. One of them licked his lips and flexed the fingers of his hand. He turned his head towards McCleod.

'Who's askin'?' he said.

'Just say a friend of Miss Sandy Kruger.'

McCleod's words had their effect. The man spun round, his face livid. Four of the other men began to fan out.

'What did you say?' the man said.

'Seems like you know the name,' McCleod

retorted. 'Perhaps you'd like to hazard a guess as to where the young lady is hidin' out from you varmints.'

The man seemed to splutter for a moment as he searched for the words and then he abandoned the effort. His hand dropped to his gun but as he drew and fired, McCleod's Colt had already spoken. He reeled backwards. McCleod was aware that the other men were drawing their weapons and he instantly spun and fired again as the man on his immediate right pulled his trigger. The two shots were almost simultaneous but it was the Cinch Buckle man who fell. Another of the Cinch Buckle men hit the floor and instinctively McCleod knew that Cherokee had drawn and fired. Two men remained standing. McCleod dropped to one knee as a bullet went screaming just over his shoulder. Before he could return fire the man went crashing backwards into one of the gaming tables as a slug from Cherokee's six-gun tore into his chest. Shots were ricocheting round the room and most of the people in the saloon had either flung themselves to the floor or were cowering behind overturned tables. Smoke hung like a curtain and the noise was deafening. Although his ears were ringing, McCleod became aware of a loud desperate shout and realized that the remaining Cinch Buckle man was calling for him and Cherokee to stop shooting. His finger was already closing on the trigger and he swung the gun up so that his shot went thudding into the ceiling. After a moment there was a shattering crash as a chandelier fell. Glass bounced along the floor and one of the girls screamed. Then there was a silence almost as palpable as the sound of gunfire had been. McCleod sprang back to his feet and advanced on the one gunnie left standing.

'Throw your gun aside!' he snapped.

The man was holding his hands in the air and allowed the six-gun to slip from his grasp. The noise of it hitting the floor seemed to bring the place back to life.

'What the hell was that all about?' the barman said.

'You saw. They made the first move.'

McCleod looked round to check on Cherokee.

'You OK?' he called.

'Sure. Arm's been grazed, nothin' more. How about you?'

'Yeah. I'm fine.'

McCleod and Cherokee were standing shoulder to shoulder. They looked about the room, making sure that no one felt inclined to take the issue further.

'Better get a doctor,' McCleod said.

He couldn't be sure whether any of the men they had shot were still alive and he didn't intend staying around to find out. Together, he and Cherokee began to back out of the saloon. Once they were through the batwings they climbed quickly into leather. A small crowd had gathered on the opposite side to the saloon and as they galloped away they could hear a gathering noise as people began to emerge from the Tin Cup.

'Good idea to freshen up these horses,' Cherokee said. 'I figure we might need to put some distance between us and Cobb Corner.'

As they turned away from the main street they could see the figure of the marshal running towards the Tin Cup.

'Maybe we should have stayed to explain matters to the marshal,' McCleod shouted.

Cherokee shook his head.

'Better not take the chance,' he replied. 'One look at me and the marshal might get kinda prejudiced in favour of the Cinch Buckle.'

McCleod wasn't sure whether Cherokee George's cynicism was justified but he had a feeling he was probably right about not taking a chance. The marshal might have given them a favourable hearing; on the other hand, they might just have landed up in jail. One thing he felt confident about: with Cherokee George's trail skills, they wouldn't need to worry unduly about a posse ever catching up with them. That is, if the marshal decided to gather one together in the first place.

Sitting in the lounge of the Rectifying Hotel, Kruger had heard the sound of gunshots coming from somewhere outside but didn't give it much attention. In a place like Cobb Corner, incidents were bound to occur from time to time. Probably it was just some drunken bum firing off his six-gun randomly. The marshal would soon have him arrested. So when a short time later the figure of Jepson came bursting through the door with the news that three of his men had been killed and one injured in a shoot-out at the Tin Cup Saloon, he was less than happy about it.

'Higgins is in jail,' Jepson concluded. 'He was the only one unhurt.'

He paused, expecting a reply, but Kruger just sat there puffing and blowing furiously on his cigar.

'Do you want me to head down to the jailhouse and see if I can get him out?'

Kruger looked up.

'No, leave him there. What's the marshal doin' about it?'

'Nothin' much, so far as I can see.'

'Well, is he getting up a posse?'

'If he is, he ain't doin' it yet.'

Kruger was caught in two minds. One part of him wanted to get along to the marshal's office and demand action; another part of him was thinking that it might be a better idea to wash his hands of the matter. He didn't want to get involved in something that might affect his plans.

'So what happened?' he snapped. 'Who was responsible?'

In the short time he had spent at the scene of the incident, Jepson had been able to piece together what had happened, but he had no clue as to who had been involved.

'One thing the barman said,' he concluded. 'When these two varmints confronted our boys, one of 'em mentioned Miss Sandy. It didn't mean nothin' to him, but he remembered the name.'

At his words Kruger noticeably flinched. Jepson realized that he had caught his boss on a real raw spot. Again, he found himself wondering why Kruger was setting so much store in finding her.

'Get back over there, see what else you can find out,' Kruger ordered.

Jepson turned and left the room. Kruger blew out a cloud of smoke and then crushed the rest of the cigar into an ashtray. His fears were confirmed. He wasn't the only one on the trail of Miss Sandy. Yet surely there couldn't be even more people involved? After thinking about it a little further, it was his conclusion that whoever the two gunmen were, they must be the same ones that he had sent his men to kill. That could only mean they had failed. Who were these two? Was Fogle one of them? Now he had to decide whether to leave Cobb Corner immediately or carry on until the riders he had despatched to deal with them returned, assuming any of them did. Whatever he decided, he needed to get going quickly. He couldn't allow himself to fall behind in the quest for Miss Sandy.

Once she had seen the man she thought was Carl Fogle, Sandy Kruger wasted no time in making her arrangements for leaving Low Butte. Only when she had left the town behind her did she begin to reflect on her reaction. After all, would it have been so bad to meet up with Carl Fogle? She hadn't known the man particularly well but he had never done anything to upset her. His attitude towards her had been perfectly correct and she had no reason to fear him. So why had she felt it so necessary to get away and avoid him? Perhaps the way she had been treated made her wary of any approach from a man; but then she thought about McCleod and knew that wasn't true. Maybe it was just that her nerves were bad. This whole business of being pursued by Kruger had made her more sensitive than she realized. Whatever it was, it was with a huge feeling of relief that she travelled through the open country, away from the town and its terrors. She was used to driving a wagon and she felt perfectly comfortable sitting high on the driving seat with the reins in her hand. The wagon she had purchased didn't amount to much but half of it was canvas covered and it seemed to be sturdily built. She had hoped to hire one but the livery man had not been willing to let her have one on those terms – probably he expected never to see it again. Together with the two horses pulling it, it accounted for a large portion of the money she had brought away with her, but she consoled herself with the thought that when she reached her destination, she could sell it on and recoup at least part of her expenses. She had loaded it up with provisions and she had also bought a rifle; a .45 single-shot Springfield. She knew how to shoot but didn't expect to ever have to use it. Thus equipped and accoutred in her men's outfit, she was feeling confident and was beginning to enjoy herself.

The weather was beautiful. A few high clouds drifted across the sky, blown along by a gentle, soothing breeze which rippled the grass so that the prairie seemed to be alive with its own inner vitality. Some of this sense of movement and vigour communicated itself to the young woman so that she felt more alive than she had done in a long time. All her youth seemed renewed and she began to forget her difficulties. Even the clothes she was wearing began to seem comfortable and familiar. She recalled some lines from a poem she had once begun but never finished:

I heard the wind
But not its language,
I saw it move
The cottonwood branches.

The grass was bent
Where it passed by,
The clouds were blown
About the sky.

And hats and leaves
Were scattered wide
Along the streets
On every side.

The wind passed by
And didn't stay
Till it was gone
And far away.

It was a day just like today that she must have envisaged, but how much better was the real thing.

She stopped when she judged it was shortly after noon and tended to the horses before making something to eat on a portable stove. When she had finished she got out her pen and tried to write in her notebook but she felt too distracted to start anything. She felt too alive, too full of a new energy. She wanted to run and fling her arms about. Instead she began to dance and sing to herself. The grass was scattered with flowers, some of which, like goldenrod and Black-eyed Susan, she recognized, and about them all was a buzz of insects. Larks rose in the air above her and grasshoppers droned. She collected some of the wild flowers and, not knowing what to do with them when she had done so, flung them down on the bed of the wagon. She looked out across the wide expanse of prairie and the great open dome of the sky. She couldn't remember when she had last felt this way but she felt completely justified in what she had done. She wasn't apprehensive about the journey. She would go on steadily, covering the long miles, till she reached the Cinch Buckle and be united with her horse, Concho. Everything would work out well.

Cherokee George raised himself in the stirrups and surveyed their back trail. There was no sign of pursuit. He hadn't expected to see anything. They had ridden hard and taken some pains to cover their tracks. Night was drawing down and it seemed the right time to make camp and let the horses rest. He and McCleod had chosen a well concealed spot in a hollow sheltered by rocks and brush and they soon made themselves comfortable. When they had eaten and drunk their fill of hot black coffee, they lay back and smoked. The night was clear. The stars seemed close and hanging low on the horizon was a yellow moon.

'We sure taught Kruger's boys a lesson,' McCleod said. 'It was just a pity Kruger wasn't amongst them.'

'He'll be lookin' for revenge,' Cherokee replied. 'He'll be plumb mad at what happened.'

'He's gonna be madder when those others get back to town.'

'They still got Fogle and Bunce,' Cherokee replied.

McCleod looked into the flames of their campfire.

'I been thinkin' about those two,' he said.

'Thinkin'? What about?'

McCleod didn't reply immediately and when he did it was to ask a question of his own.

'Had you ever come across Fogle before this?'

'Nope.'

'Then how do you know so much about him?'

'I don't know much. Only what I learned from workin' at the Cinch Buckle and ridin' with him and Bunce.'

'I don't know. There's somethin' about him that just don't add up. You say he was a Texas Ranger. I rode with the Texas Rangers but I never come across the name. It ain't one you'd be likely to forget. Then again, I could understand Bunce endin' up dead, but someone who used to be a Texas Ranger would be unlikely to allow himself to be bushwhacked so easily. Like I said to you before, I never took him for a Texas Ranger from the start.'

'So if he ain't Fogle, who is he?'

'You said Kruger ran a gang of outlaws down on the border. You said they got split up and some of 'em ended up in the penitentiary. Kruger was the one come out with all the loot. I reckon he must have made himself a few enemies.'

'Reckon so,' Cherokee responded.

'So maybe one of 'em, maybe more than one, gets released from jail. He's been nursin' a grudge for all the time he's been caged up. When he comes out he decides it's time to get even with Kruger and claim his rightful share of the money.'

Cherokee's cigarette was finished and he began to roll himself another. He seemed unmoved by McCleod's reasoning.

'To cover his tracks, he calls himself Fogle. You say it was pretty common knowledge that Kruger ran off with Fogle's woman. When things got real nasty, he would have a good alibi. If killin' was involved, nobody would guess it was him. They would assume it was Fogle.'

'It kinda makes sense, but there's no proof. It's just as likely that Fogle was who he said he was.'

'No,' McCleod retorted. 'Not if we take into account what I was just sayin' about our so-called Texas Ranger friend. And there's one other thing. Somehow, the man calling himself Fogle knew that I'd worked for Kruger in the days when he ran the Hog Eye. He might have got that from you. I said it was down in the San Catrudos River country. The Hog Eye weren't anywhere near there. For somebody seemin' to know as much as he did, that was a big error.'

Cherokee suddenly let out a low grunt that McCleod interpreted as a laugh.

'Hell,' he said, 'what difference does it make? Whether Fogle was who he said he was or not, he's dead now.'

'That's right. But Kruger would have assumed he was the real Fogle. If I'm anywhere near bein' right about this, the real Fogle could be still be around somewhere. Especially if you're right about him puttin' himself back together after he hit the slide.'

They lapsed into silence until McCleod added one more thought:

'That still leaves open the question why everyone seems to be so keen on locating Miss Sandy. And we won't know that till we find her.'

'Or until somebody else does,' Cherokee replied. 'But in that case I suppose we would never get to know.'

McCleod glanced across at him.

'You talk too much,' he said.

While McCleod and Cherokee George were able to enjoy a night spent out in the open under the stars, the same was not true of Miss Sandy. By the time the evening shadows had spread across the land her former feeling of pleasure and elation had faded away. She drew up in the shade of some cottonwood trees by a pool of water and set about trying to make herself comfortable for the night, but it was not a task she relished. She managed to build a fire and get some water from the pool to make coffee but when night finally descended she felt too scared to remain in the open. Kicking out the remains of the fire she had built, she crept back into the shelter of the canvas cover of her wagon. She ate some cold beans out of a can but she wasn't hungry. For a while she tried to write something but could not concentrate. She took up a book and instead tried to read but the words meant nothing. When she had read the same sentence a number of times without it making any sense to her, she put the book down and pulled her blanket up around her shoulders. The light from her lantern cast flickering shadows on the canvas and her imagination began to conjure up various phantoms. The wind sounded ghostly as it rustled the cottonwood leaves and the rippling of the stream provided a sinister accompaniment. Presently she blew out the light and cowered in the darkness. The night was full of strange sounds and then from somewhere further away there rose the chilling howl of a coyote. She got to her feet and, opening the canvas flap an inch or two, peered out into the darkness. A strange pallor illumined the night as if a shroud had been cast over the landscape. She looked up. A big moon cast its silvery beams and a myriad stars hung like silver pieces in the velvet sky. She could see a long way across the rolling land. It looked so empty. She began to think of McCleod. If only he was here. How wonderful it would be to be able to trust somebody, to feel the security of someone's care and protection. Closing the gap in the canvas, she reached up for the Springfield rifle but it provided her with only a hollow illusion of safety. Laying it by her side, she stretched out once more on her bedroll and waited anxiously for the first signs of dawn.

McCleod woke with a start. He lay without moving, listening for any sound, but there was nothing he could hear that was not to be expected; just the breeze soughing and the occasional stamp of a hoof. He turned his head. Cherokee was lying away from the last flickering embers of the fire in the shadow of a rock. He knew that if there had been anything untoward in the night, Cherokee would have wakened. He couldn't get back to sleep and rose instead. He walked a few yards out of the circle of the fire and looked out across the prairie. He felt in his pocket for his tobacco and felt the rustle of paper. The night had a strange translucency about it and he could almost see to read Sandy's letter. Rolling a cigarette, he peered at it in the added light it provided.

Phantoms flit
Across the lawn;
Some tattered leaves
The wind has torn.

While from a branch

Of the shadowed beech
The pale moon hangs
Just out of reach.

The child's asleep:
Now nothing seems
Quite so real
As in his dreams.

When he got to the end of the poem, he paused to reflect. The moon shining over the prairie was not pale but it certainly seemed to hang almost within reach, and he could almost imagine that the shapes and dim forms he could see were phantoms running not across the lawn, but across the immense open grasslands. Had Miss Sandy ever seen a lawn or was it some poetical image she had taken from her reading?

There was something unreal, too, about the night and the wide landscape. Was Miss Sandy asleep and dreaming? She wasn't much more than a child herself. How would she be coping with her situation? She seemed to have made a pretty good job of things in Cobb Corner, but something had scared her and made her run again. He could only hope that he was right and that she had taken the stage in the direction of Low Butte. His thoughts reverted to his previous conversation with Cherokee George. It was obvious that Miss Sandy held the secret which was driving Kruger to seek her out. If he was right about Fogle, and he was one of Kruger's former gang, there could be only one fundamental reason why he would seek him out. Revenge was obviously a factor, but it must be money he was after. Kruger had taken the loot and bought first the Hog Eye and then the Cinch Buckle. Maybe there was more of it somewhere and the clue to its whereabouts lay with Miss Sandy. There had to be a lot of it, too, to warrant all the fuss and commotion, and it had to be somewhere even Kruger didn't know. What could Miss Sandy possibly have that they all wanted? Presumably she was unaware herself that she carried the secret. Suddenly he found himself thinking about Fogle's woman, the one who had run off with Kruger. Cherokee had said that she had died. Was that recently? What had she died of? He felt he was on to something and glanced back at Cherokee George. He was undecided about waking him. Maybe this could all wait till morning when he would have had more time to think about it. He hesitated, but then turned and knelt down beside the sleeping form of his companion. As he did so Cherokee's eyes flickered open and McCleod found himself staring into the muzzle of a Colt Dragoon.

'Don't do that again,' Cherokee snapped.

'Put it down,' McCleod said. 'I need to talk.'

Cherokee slipped the gun back under his blanket. 'I thought we'd done all that,' he said.

'Listen,' McCleod said. 'This might be important. You said that Fogle's woman, the one Kruger ran off with, died and that left Miss Sandy way out on a limb. When did this happen? Was it recently?'

'Sure. Not more than a few months ago.'

'What caused her death?' McCleod said.

Cherokee shrugged.

'I don't know. All I heard is that she died.'

'Was the death investigated?'

'Not that I know of. There were some rumours but I didn't take no notice of them.'

'Rumours?'

'Nothin' in particular. Guess that's just the way things are. Somebody dies unexpectedly, people talk.'

'So it was unexpected. That's interestin'.'

McCleod was trying to organise his chaotic thoughts.

'What if Miss Sandy suspected somethin'? What if she saw somethin'? Kruger would have good cause to want her out of the way.'

'She would have done somethin' straight off,' Cherokee replied. 'It was only later that she ran away.'

'Yeah. I guess that can't be it.'

McCleod was using Cherokee as a sounding board for his ideas. He felt he was getting close to something but it was still all guesswork.

'Kruger bought the Hog Eye first and then the Cinch Buckle. Neither of those spreads would be goin' cheap. You say he used to run cattle across the Mexican border. He would need to do a lot of cattle rustlin' to make that sort of money. It would take a lot more to run them. What if he was runnin' out of money but then found out after all the time he had been livin' with her that Fogle's woman had money of her own?'

Cherokee got to his feet and flung a few branches on the fire.

'I don't know about you,' he said, 'but I could do with more coffee. All this talk ain't gettin' us anywhere. It's all just pie in the sky. Seems to me the best thing is to let it rest and get started on the trail to Low Butte just as quick as we can.'

McCleod sighed.

'You're right,' he said. 'I guess my brain is just gettin' plumb heated. The one certain thing is that we must find Miss Sandy before anyone else. She's the important thing. Once we've found her, maybe the rest will fit into place.'

While they drank the coffee he couldn't help speculating further. It was all a whirl. When they eventually swung into leather and hit the trail, it was a relief to be back in action again.

CHAPTER FIVE

Kruger stepped out of the stage depot at Superstition in bright sunlight but his face was dark with anger and frustration. It was too early yet to be sure that Miss Sandy had escaped him again; he had sent his men into each of the small towns they had passed along the way to check on whether she had left the stage at that point and some of them had yet to report to him. Still, it was not looking good. He made his way to the nearest saloon and took a table near the batwings. A girl approached him but he waved her aside. After a few moments the batwings swung open and Jepson came in and joined him.

'Well?' Kruger snapped.

'No sign of her at the hotel. I checked the names in the hotel register and had a word with the clerk. He didn't recognize my description.'

'Did you talk to the town marshal?'

'Yeah. I told him Miss Sandy was a runaway but he hasn't seen or heard anythin' around town.'

Kruger swore beneath his breath.

'Just wait till I get my hands on the minx,' he said. 'I'll teach her to run off and cause all this trouble.'

Jepson looked closely at his boss. Now wasn't a good time to say what was on his mind but he spoke anyway.

'Why go to all theses lengths to find Miss Sandy?' he said. 'Sooner or later she'll probably get tired of the whole business and come right back to where she started from. Why don't we all just go back to the Cinch Buckle? She'll turn up soon enough.'

Kruger gave him a withering look.

'I don't pay you for your opinions,' he said. 'She's got to be somewhere. Get back out there and take a look around. Meet me back here in two hours' time.'

Jepson got to his feet and shuffled out. Why should he worry about it? He had two hours to himself. Long enough to sample whatever the town had to offer.

Left to his own devices, Kruger weighed up the possibilities. He had it on good evidence that Miss Sandy had caught the stage at Cobb Corner. It seemed she had not got off at any of the towns between Cobb Corner and Superstition. They had checked out the few way-stations *en route.* That left two possibilities. Either she had got off and somehow carried on her journey by other means, or she had taken the stage in the opposite direction. He cursed again. It had been a considerable ride and he had been put to a lot of inconvenience. The only good news so far had been the reported shooting of Fogle and whoever else had been riding with him. He couldn't be completely sure that it was Fogle who had tracked Miss Sandy to Cobb Corner but it seemed a pretty fair bet. That was one irritant out of his way. He glanced up. The girl who had approached his table was still standing by the bar and returned his look. She wasn't especially attractive but she was young. He deserved a bit of fun. She wasn't anything like Miss Sandy but she would do. He gave a slight nod of the head and in a few moments she joined him. He ordered a bottle of brandy and a couple of glasses and then followed her as she led the way up the stairs to a sparsely furnished room on the floor above.

For several days Miss Sandy had not seen a living soul and she began to be aware of how huge the open prairie was. The vast distances all around her made her light headed. She still felt a degree of fear when night fell but she was beginning to get accustomed to it. She had got into a habit of talking to the horses. She had become quite adept at looking after herself and appeared to be making good progress. Sometimes she got down from the wagon seat and walked. Only occasionally did she think about Kruger. She was looking forward to reaching her destination and being reunited with Concho. She had something definite to aim for. What she would do after that was of little concern to her for the moment.

The weather had been fine but towards noon of the fifth day the sky began to darken. Banks of cloud had come up from the west and the wind, changing direction from southwest to northeast, began to increase in strength quite suddenly. All around the prairie grass waved and danced so that there seemed to be nothing firm or solid, and the rushing wail of the wind grew louder until it reverberated in Sandy's ears like a drum. As if in reply, bursts of thunder began to roll across the sky while forked lightning snaked and streaked across it with lurid, vivid slashes of light. The thunder and lightning continued but for a moment the wind relented and there followed a strange hiatus. Miss Sandy looked up at the darkened sky. Suddenly the air was filled with a white fury and she instinctively turned away as a great ball of ice struck her on the shoulder. Accompanied by redoubled peals of thunder, the hailstorm broke over her with tremendous energy.

Maddened by pain, the horses backed and reared, wheeling their heads from the storm. Miss Sandy jumped to the ground, struggling to get them under control. She was knocked to the ground but picked herself up again. There was a loud cracking, rending noise as the wagon tongue broke; there had been some danger of the wagon being pulled right over but now the struggling of the beasts lessened and they seemed to calm down a little. Overhead the thunder boomed while the hailstorm continued unabated, tearing at any exposed flesh. Some of the hailstones were larger than a walnut, rebounding and ricocheting from firm surfaces and tearing at the cloth of the wagon cover. Desperately, she sought shelter beneath the wagon, cowering in terror and dismay. The noise of the hail striking the ground was an unrestrained chamade. It seemed to Sandy that the storm would never cease, but as quickly as it had begun it drew to a close. The hailstones thinned and the hailstorm turned into a torrential rain which began to quickly slacken. The thunder and lightning passed further down the sky till Sandy felt it was safe to emerge.

She expected the worst. It seemed impossible that she should have endured such a convulsion of nature without the wagon suffering serious damage, and so it proved. The wagon cover was ripped and torn, but more seriously, the wagon tongue had broken. Soaked through, feeling bruised and battered, Sandy sank to the ground in despair. This was something she had not bargained for and she did not know what to do about it. She realized how thoughtless she had been. Carried aloft by a wave of confidence and enthusiasm, she had failed to plan properly. As the storm drifted away towards the horizon and she looked about her at the ravaged landscape, she had another sickening realization. She was lost. She looked for anything distinctive in the prospect but wherever her eyes searched they found the same undifferentiated wilderness. Despite her troubles, so far she had been able to keep up a determined outlook. Now, for the first time in a long while, she couldn't help but break into sobs of bitter anguish. She was lost and the wagon was useless. It was a hopeless situation.

As the sun began to warm the drenched prairie and dry her sodden garments, she began to feel a little better. She did her best to tend to the horses and then climbed up on the wagon to ascertain how much damage had been done to her equipment and supplies. They were in a bad way. She lifted the rifle and put it down again, not knowing whether it would still be in working order. Then she suddenly let out an involuntary gasp. What about her notebooks? For a frantic moment she scrabbled about among the debris in the wagon, when she remembered that she had put them in a small japanned box. She poked about among the wreckage but couldn't see it. The wagon was tilted over and some of the things she had stored had slipped out. Leaning over the back of the wagon, she saw the box lying amidst a jumble of her possessions. At least her notebooks were safe. Her care in storing them was justified.

When she had done what she could to restore some semblance of order in the wagon, she set about building a fire. She was feeling hungry and cooked some beans and bacon. She made coffee and all the while she was thinking about what to do next. By the time she had finished her meal, she had come to a decision. It was getting dark. She would stay for the night where she was and next day see if there was any way she could repair the wagon. If she couldn't do so, she would saddle one of the horses and use the other as a pack horse to carry whatever supplies she could retrieve. She would have to carry her notebooks in one of the saddle-bags. They wouldn't be as protected as they had been in the box, but she would have to do the best she could.

*

When McCleod and Cherokee George rode into Low Butte it didn't take them long to work out that Miss Sandy wasn't there. She would have to be staying at the hotel or one of the lodging houses and there weren't many of them. As an extra precaution, McCleod paid a call on the marshal. It was his experience that the town marshal usually had a pretty good idea about the comings and goings locally; he assured them that so far as he was aware, no young lady answering to Miss Sandy's description had been seen around the place.

'However,' he concluded, 'I reckon it's kinda strange that you're the second person been askin' about this young lady.'

'What do you mean?' McCleod asked.

'Just what I say. You're the second person that's come through my door askin' the same question. Now I'd say that was a real coincidence, wouldn't you?'

'When was this?'

'Let me think for a moment. Not more than three days. Yes, that's right. It woulda been day before yesterday.'

'Did he give his name?'

'Nope, and I didn't ask him. Didn't need to.'

'What did he look like?'

By way of reply, the marshal reached into a drawer and took out a folded poster.

'He looked like this,' he replied. 'A little bit older,

a little bit more lined, but it's the same man.'

He handed it to McCleod. Even as he unfolded it McCleod had an inkling of who it would be.

'Fogle,' he said. 'Carl Fogle.'

'That's an old Wanted poster,' the marshal said. 'Fogle's done his time. But you never can tell when an outdated dodger like that might come in useful.'

McCleod was thinking to himself that Fogle had fallen further since his time as a Texas Ranger than anyone had even allowed for.

'Where's Fogle now?' he asked.

The marshal gestured towards a cell at the back of the office.

'He almost ended up in there,' he said.

McCleod looked puzzled.

'There was an incident in the saloon. Seemed like he got into some sort of fracas with another drifter. I told them both to get out of town.'

McCleod was thinking fast. If Fogle had been involved in a fight, it probably meant that at least one of Kruger's men had made his way to Low Butte. That was unfortunate, even if it remained the case that Kruger himself, together with the majority of his riders, had left Cobb Corner in the direction of Superstition.

'Are you plannin' to stay long in town?' the marshal asked.

'Nope. Just passin' through,' McCleod replied.

He was already making for the door when the marshal commented:

'Whoever this Miss Sandy is, she sure seems to have a heap of admirers.'

McCleod closed the door behind him and made for the saloon where he had left Cherokee George. Apart from the necessity to find Miss Sandy as quickly as possible, he was anxious to avoid any complications arising from the possibility of his friend getting into trouble again. Fortunately that gentleman seemed to have similar ideas because he emerged from the saloon even before McCleod had reached it.

'Let's not waste time,' McCleod said as they stepped into leather. 'Seems like I was right about Fogle. The real one, that is. He was here but he's left. And he's ahead of us.'

They rode quickly away from Low Butte, heading for the open prairie. As they left they passed the livery stable where the ostler watched them go. If he had known who they were, or if they had stopped to question him, he would have been able to enlighten them. He still sometimes thought about the young lady who had bought the wagon and horses. It still seemed strange to him that a young woman would want to travel alone. She was putting herself into a position of some danger, but he supposed she knew what she was doing.

Kruger deliberated long about getting back in the saddle before he eventually chose to ride out of Superstition with his Cinch Buckle hands. He was getting a bit old for all this range riding and he was tempted to make himself comfortable at the hotel and enjoy the various delights the town had to offer.

In the end his presentiment that there was too much at stake to be put at any risk persuaded him that he needed to be present when Miss Sandy was finally discovered. His experience of his men's deficiencies made him unable to rely on them entirely. And if he was right in his belief that they would find something important when they came to search her belongings, it would be necessary to be able to follow it up without delay. That was the main reason he had brought so many of his outfit along with him. He had a feeling that they would be needed. There had been no sign of Miss Sandy at any of the towns his men had stopped off at. He had despatched some of them to ride on hard ahead and check out the towns going in the opposite direction from Cobb Corner. He didn't like to think that Miss Sandy had outfoxed him, but it was beginning to look that way. If she wasn't at any of those places, then they would scour the prairie until they found her.

The night was dark and cloudy. Gathered about several scattered camp-fires Kruger's gunnies were black smudges in the smoky gloom. As he sat on a camp-stool, Kruger was shaken from his reveries by the thud of approaching hoof beats. A couple of his men got to their feet with their rifles in their hands, but it was only Jepson riding into camp. The guards put down their weapons; Jepson jumped from his horse and approached Kruger.

'Where have you been?' the latter snapped.

Jepson sat down and poured himself a mug of coffee.

'Well?' Kruger repeated.

'I got to feelin' restless,' Jepson replied. 'Figured I'd take a little ride. Ain't much of a night for it but I reckon you're gonna thank me that I did.'

'Stop beatin' about the bush,' Kruger replied.

'I rode out quite a ways,' Jepson said. 'I was just about to turn back when I thought I saw somethin' a ways off. I rode on and made a discovery. It was a broken-down wagon.'

Kruger was suddenly attentive, but then relapsed into his mood of irritable distraction.

'There's probably plenty of wagons scattered about the prairie,' he said. 'You findin' one don't mean anythin'.'

'Maybe so, but I think not. Although it's dark I took a look at the wagon and made a strange discovery. Among various other things that'd been left behind, I found some discarded clothes. Women's clothes. Now ain't that a strange thing?'

'Women's clothes?'

'Might not mean anythin', but I figured it could just be significant.'

'What? You reckon they could belong to Miss Sandy? Did you recognize any of 'em?'

Jepson shook his head.

'How far is this wagon?' Kruger said.

'About five miles away.'

Kruger was thinking.

'OK,' he concluded. 'There's probably nothing in this, but it could be worth investigatin'. It won't take long and it's not as if we got a definite route in mind.

Get some sleep. In the mornin' we'll go take a closer look, see what else we can find in daylight.'

Jepson got to his feet.

'You done a good job,' Kruger said. 'I won't forget it.'

When he had gone Kruger drew a cigar out of his pocket which he trimmed and then lighted. The more he thought about what Jepson had told him, the more he liked it. Perhaps it didn't amount to anything. On the other hand, it could be just the break they were looking for.

Miss Sandy had no better plan than to try and ride consistently in one direction. She wasn't sure which way the Cinch Buckle was but she set off in the direction she thought it would be. She knew she had a long ride ahead of her. She rode steadily, letting her horse go at its own pace and leading the second horse. The weather was improving after the storm but she was wearing a slicker. She had been taught a lesson about how quickly it could change. She had a renewed sense of the vastness of her surroundings and her corresponding insignificance. If anything happened to her, she might never be found. She fell to reflecting whether, if that happened, anyone would even miss her. Kruger might but for all the wrong reasons. Would anyone miss her for herself? She tried to put such thoughts from her mind and concentrate on what she was doing. She was glad she had swapped her clothes for those of a man. Now that she was used to them they made riding a lot more comfortable. She was a good rider. The two horses she had at her disposal, both duns, were not especially good ones but she figured that if she nursed them along and gave them proper care and attention, they would do. A long way ahead she could make out the vague outline of some low-lying hills and decided to set her course by them. She felt less concerned about being lost than she had when she first realized it. She reckoned that if she kept going in a particular direction, even if it was the wrong one, she must arrive somewhere. Either she would come across a ranch or a shack, a settlement of some kind, or maybe just another rider. There was no need to panic. She just had to keep a level head. So she rode on, directing her course towards the hills.

Late in the afternoon she rode down into a creek bottom. After the rains, it was running high. She stopped to let the horses drink and fill her canteens. Along the banks she saw tracks which she was fairly sure were those of deer and antelope. She mounted again and carried on for a while before riding back up on the flats. All of a sudden the hills seemed closer. They were not high, more like a series of swelling ridges. She hadn't gone much further when she thought she saw movement. Pulling the dun to a halt, she put her hand to her eyes to shield them from the westering sun. There was a glint of light and then she saw something move against the backdrop of the rising ground to her left. It was a rider. Her heart thumped and she gave an audible sigh of relief.

'There you are,' she said to the dun. 'Didn't I tell

you that if we just kept on going we'd be OK, we'd find something or somebody?'

She couldn't tell whether the rider had seen her, but she didn't hesitate. Applying her spurs, she urged the horses into a canter. The rider had now changed direction and it was clear that he had seen her too. The distance between them rapidly lessened and she could see him quite clearly now. Suddenly her euphoria evaporated. There was something about him that looked vaguely familiar. She thought back to her first sighting of the man she thought was a Cinch Buckle rider back in Cobb Corner. She couldn't be sure, but she had a feeling it was the same man. Whether it was or not, she was suddenly scared. Even if it wasn't, who was he and what was he doing out here? Hadn't she been a fool to assume that he would be friendly. Her experience of the storm and of being lost had undermined her self-confidence and she had been too quick to assume that rescue was at hand. Then she remembered the way she was dressed. She was wearing a man's clothing. Maybe, if the man proved hostile, she might yet get away unscathed. She pulled her hat low and huddled down in her slicker.

The rider came alongside her.

'Howdy,' she said.

'Howdy,' the man replied.

She could see now that the horse he was riding was carrying a Cinch Buckle brand. The man looked at her and then scratched his chin.

'Don't suppose you seen a bunch of riders any

place?' Sandy continued.

'A bunch of riders?' the man repeated.

'Yeah. Four of 'em. We was lookin' for somebody. Found his pack horse. The others might have split up.'

'Nope,' the man said. 'Ain't seen nobody.'

'I'd best get on,' she replied.

She was about to move past him when he spoke again.

'Now that's kinda funny,' he said. 'I just been to Thorpeville lookin' for somebody myself. A woman. She ain't there.'

'Ain't seen no woman,' Sandy said.

'Nope. Guess she's probably in Superstition or someplace by now.'

'Well, I hope you find her,' Sandy replied.

She urged her horse forward once more and carried on up the trail. She had to fight an inclination to look back. She had tried to speak as low as she could and to take the initiative by mentioning some non-existent riders, hoping to deter the man from taking too much interest in her by doing so. As she rode she listened attentively for any sounds of hoofs in her rear but the man seemed to have continued on his way. After riding a little further she could no longer resist the temptation and took a quick look backward. The man was quite a long distance away. She suddenly found that she was trembling. It had been a close run thing and she was surprised that she had had the nerve to pull it off. Now a reaction set in and she had to stop and get down from the dun. She sat down on the grass and put her head in her hands. For some time she remained that way till she felt strong enough to resume her journey. She climbed back into the saddle. At least she had learned two things: that so far she had failed to throw off Kruger and that there was a town called Thorpeville somewhere not too far away. Looking back, she could see no sign of the Cinch Buckle rider.

It didn't take long for Kruger and Jepson to find Sandy's abandoned wagon when they rode out in the early morning. Kruger immediately knew that it was hers. He recognized some of her clothing and other items, but he couldn't see the one thing he was looking for.

'I want this thing turned upside down!' he barked.

'What are we searchin' for?' Jepson replied.

'You're lookin' for a box containing some notebooks. They belong to Miss Sandy. She writes things, poems and such-like. They might be loose but it's more likely she keeps 'em in a box. Be careful not to cause any damage and bring 'em to me as soon as you find 'em.'

Even as he spoke the words, however, he knew that they wouldn't find what he was looking for. Those notebooks were Miss Sandy's most treasured possession. Even in her current desperate circumstances she wouldn't leave them behind. It didn't matter too much, however, because he knew that he was fast closing in on her. It was obvious what had happened. She couldn't be far away now and she wouldn't get much further. It was only a question of time, and a very little time, before he located her. It was a stroke of luck that Jepson had found the wagon, but in any event she couldn't have held out much longer. He had a feeling that his problems were about to be solved.

McCleod had confidence in Cherokee George. He was certain that if Miss Sandy had left the stagecoach somewhere to make her own way, Cherokee would find her. Now, as they splashed through a creek, Cherokee drew to a halt and held up his hand.

'I had a feelin' that Miss Sandy might have come this way.'

He pointed towards the left-hand bank.

'Take a look,' he said.

McCleod turned his head. There were several animal tracks but a little further along, he saw the tracks of two riders. They rode up to them.

'Two riders,' McCleod said. 'What do you think? A couple of Kruger's men?'

'Have a closer look,' Cherokee replied.

McCleod dismounted. There were definitely two sets of tracks, one a little ahead of the other. At no place did they come side by side. Suddenly McCleod realized there were not two riders, but one rider leading a pack horse.

'The first set of tracks is different from the other set,' Cherokee said, 'because the first horse carried a rider and the second didn't.'

McCleod looked again. Cherokee was right. The first tracks were slightly more indented and the horses' hoofs were differently planted. He swung back into the saddle.

'What do you make of them?' he said.

Cherokee glanced about him.

'I don't know,' he said.

'I don't imagine they've got anythin' to do with Miss Sandy,' McCleod replied. 'Hell, it would be a helluva long shot.'

'You're right,' Cherokee replied. 'But whoever made those tracks, they ain't too far ahead. Allowin' for the fact it's unlikely to be Miss Sandy, maybe whoever made 'em could tell us somethin' that might come in useful.'

'Like he's seen Miss Sandy? Like he knows where she's stayin'? That's about as likely as findin' Miss Sandy herself.'

Cherokee shrugged in his customary fashion.

'OK, you're right,' McCleod said. 'What have we got to lose? Let's carry on and follow the tracks. We've been more or less headin' in that direction anyway.'

As they rode along the swollen stream-bed, McCleod had no difficulty following the sign where the muddy banks of the stream showed it fairly clearly, but when they rode up on to the plain he had to rely on Cherokee. It was midday and the low hills which had showed as a hazy blue sheen earlier were close now and revealed their contours. They rode up a long stretch of rising ground that looked out over a great sweep of prairie extending to the broken country in the direction of Marmot Wallow, but they didn't stop to admire the view. They were both conscious that this time they could be on to something. Then, just a little further on, in a sheltered spot, they came on the remnants of a camp-fire.

'Only one person has been here,' Cherokee said. 'One person, two horses. And they ain't been left long.'

The sign was obvious now and they didn't pause. Urging their horses into a gallop, they covered the ground rapidly till, cresting another rise, they had their first sight of their quarry. Keeping just below the level of the hill, McCleod drew out his field glasses and, guarding against making a reflection, concentrated them on the figure of the rider.

'It ain't Miss Sandy,' he said.

Even though he realized that the chances of the unknown rider being her were very slim, he still couldn't help feeling a strong sense of disappointment. He passed the glasses to Cherokee George who took a close look.

'Do you reckon it could be one of Kruger's men?'

'Maybe, but I don't see any special reason to think it. I guess it's just some *hombre* passin' through to somewhere.'

'There's only one way to find out,' Cherokee replied.

McCleod replaced the glasses in their holder and they mounted up.

'OK, let's catch him up. Like you said, maybe he can give us some information at least.'

They rode down the slope from the crest of the hill. The distance between themselves and the rider rapidly lessened but it wasn't till they were quite close that the rider became aware of their presence. When Sandy heard their galloping hoofs, she turned to face them, fearful that it was the Cinch Buckle rider. For a moment she thought it might still be him, together with another of Kruger's men, and steeled herself for a further confrontation. As the two horsemen got near, her attitude changed. She could see that it was not the Cinch Buckle man but as yet she did not recognize McCleod. The two riders came to a halt beside her.

'Howdy,' McCleod said.

Something about his grizzled features reminded her of somebody and his voice sounded strangely familiar.

'Guess we rode up kinda sudden. Hope we didn't scare you none.'

McCleod paused, looking more closely at the rider's features.

'We were . . .' he continued and then stopped. The rider's eyes were open wide with an expression of astonishment.

'McCleod,' Sandy gasped. 'Is it you? It can't be.'

The look on her face was mirrored by McCleod as the truth suddenly dawned on him.

'Miss Sandy!' he exclaimed.

The next moment they had both jumped from their horses and McCleod was holding Sandy in his arms. Cherokee watched, but if he was surprised his features did not show it. Sandy clung closely to McCleod and her shoulders shook. After a time

McCleod held her at arm's length to look more closely at her face. There were tears in her eyes but the sobbing had stopped. She looked up at him and the beginnings of a smile lifted the corners of her mouth.

'McCleod! McCleod!' she repeated. 'Oh, I'm so glad you are here. How did you know? I can't believe it's really you.'

McCleod glanced at Cherokee, who only now had dismounted. He felt that the time had come to calm things down.

'Miss Sandy,' he said. 'I'd like you to meet my friend Cherokee George. It's largely thanks to him that we found you.'

Miss Sandy looked slightly askance at Cherokee.

'Cherokee, Miss Sandy Kruger,' McCleod concluded.

Cherokee George took Miss Sandy's awkwardly extended hand and shook it.

'Mighty nice to meet you, ma'am,' he said.

McCleod looked Miss Sandy up and down.

'For a moment or two there you almost had me fooled,' he said. 'What on earth are you doin' wearin' those duds?'

Miss Sandy glanced down at herself and then began to laugh.

'What do you think? Do I look the part?'

McCleod laughed too.

'Depends what part you're tryin' to play,' he replied.

There was a pause and they suddenly felt a little awkward.

'I reckon we should make camp,' McCleod said. 'I don't think anyone's in a hurry to get any place and I reckon there's a power of explainin' to be done all round.'

'Yes,' Miss Sandy replied. 'That would be nice.'

Having to do something helped to relieve any tension which might have arisen and by the time they had shared the duties of gathering fuel, building a fire, cooking some food, boiling coffee and tending to the horses, they were feeling a lot more relaxed and comfortable with one another. When they had eaten Miss Sandy was ready to talk. When McCleod heard about the part Kruger had played in her account, he grew angry.

'Are you tellin' us the whole story?' he asked.

Miss Sandy nodded her head.

'Yes. He tried to . . . he tried to. . . .'

'It's OK,' McCleod replied. He put his hand out and touched her shoulder.

'Hey,' he said, 'What about those poems? I been tellin' Cherokee all about them. Are you still writin'?'

Miss Sandy smiled nervously.

'Yes,' she said. 'In fact, I don't know what I'd have done if I hadn't had my notebooks.'

'Maybe you can show me some of them later,' McCleod replied.

'I'd like that. But you haven't said what you're doin' here? I haven't seen you for two years. Did you get my letter?'

'Sure.'

He reached into his pocket and drew out the letter

with the poem she had written for him. He began to explain how he had become involved and the events leading up to Cherokee and him finding her. As he spoke he occasionally looked to Cherokee who added some details to the story. When he had finished they sat for some time in silence, each trying to digest what the other had said.

'Poor Roy!' Miss Sandy said. 'I didn't realize—'

'It's all right. It was his choice to go lookin' for you.'

Evening shadows were creeping over the hills. Miss Sandy, putting memories of Bunce behind her, began to think what a difference it was camping out now that McCleod was here. Before, the coming of night had brought fear and menace. Now she felt warm and secure.

'You don't mind if we smoke?' McCleod asked her.

'No, of course not.'

McCleod rolled a cigarette and handed the makings to Cherokee. When they had lit up Miss Sandy turned again to McCleod.

'I don't know if I did the wrong thing to run away from the Cinch Buckle,' she said, 'but there's one thing I can't understand.'

'You didn't do the wrong thing,' McCleod replied. 'There's no reason to blame yourself for anythin'. What is it you don't understand?'

'Well, I don't understand why Mr Kruger would go to such lengths to try and trace me. I would have thought that he wouldn't be too concerned.'

McCleod was glad that Miss Sandy had brought up

the topic herself. It was the question which had been worrying him.

'Yes,' he replied. 'It does seem kinda strange. Me and Cherokee have been wonderin' about that too.'

'And can you or Mr Cherokee think of a reason?'

McCleod paused to inhale the tobacco.

'We've had some discussions. The best we can come up with is that you must have somethin' that Kruger wants. And it must be something pretty important. The only thing we can think of is that maybe it's got somethin' to do with your poems, with your notebooks.'

'My poems? How could that be?'

'I don't know.'

McCleod offered to pour Miss Sandy another cup of coffee but she shook her head. He could see in the light of the fire that she was looking worn.

'Well,' he said, 'I reckon we could all do with some shuteye. Why don't we leave it till the morning? Maybe after a good night's sleep we'll all be able to think straight.'

'I am feeling tired,' Miss Sandy commented.

Cherokee got to his feet.

'I'll make up your bed, Miss Sandy,' he said.

When he had gone to the horses, Miss Sandy stretched out and laid her head on McCleod's shoulder.

'I'm so glad you found me,' she said.

'So am I,' he replied.'You've had a hard time, but from now on you're safe. Don't worry about nothin'. Just rest.'

In the short time that it took for Cherokee to make up the bed, Miss Sandy had dozed off. Carefully, McCleod lifted her up and carried her over to her bedroll. He placed her gently down and covered her with blankets. Then he kissed her on the brow before getting up and returning to his place by the fire.

'She is a resourceful young woman,' Cherokee commented.

'Yeah. And she's also a child,' McCleod replied.

'Whatever you plan on doin' next, I reckon we'd better get movin'.'

'Why do say that?'

'Because when that *hombre* Miss Sandy met on the trail gets back to Kruger, he ain't gonna waste no time in comin' lookin' for us.'

McCleod thought for a moment.

'Yeah, of course.'

He looked towards the sleeping shape of Miss Sandy.

'She'll be fine once she's had a good night's rest. She'll be ready to start off early in the mornin'.'

'Why don't you get some sleep as well? I'll go on watch.'

McCleod was feeling pretty tired himself.

'OK,' he replied. 'But be sure you wake me up half way through to do my stint.'

Cherokee wandered off to take up a position where he had a clear view of their back trail. The night was moonless but it made little difference to him. He could see in the dark like a wild cat.

McCleod lay down at a little distance from the fire but although he tried, he could not get to sleep. All the while his brain was puzzling over the question of what it could be that Kruger was after. He felt sure that the answer lay with Miss Sandy. Still trying to work it out, he eventually fell into a fitful slumber.

CHAPTER SIX

He awoke to find the first streaks of dawn painting the sky. The fire had been built up and he heard the sound of sizzling bacon. He looked up to see Miss Sandy leaning over the flames.

'Good morning,' she said. 'Breakfast will be ready soon.'

He got to his feet and looked about him.

'Where's Cherokee?' he said.

She pointed in the direction of the horses.

'Feeding them,' she replied.

'He was supposed to wake me up,' he said.

When breakfast was finished and they were enjoying the first cup of coffee, McCleod thought it was time to bring up the matter of Kruger and his pursuit of Miss Sandy.

'I've been thinking about this a lot, and it seems to me that it must involve your papers. Somewhere among your writings is the thing Kruger is so keen to lay his hands on.'

Miss Sandy nodded.

'Yes, I think you're right. Let me go and get my notebooks.'

She got to her feet and went to look in her saddle-bags. In a few moments she was back with a bundle of papers. They were looking slightly more crumpled than they had previously.

'Have you been keeping them in your saddle-bags? You can't have because you said you hired most of your equipment in Low Butte.'

'No. I had to put them in the saddle-bags after I got caught in the storm.'

'Where were they before that?'

'I kept them in a tin box.'

'Where did you find the box?'

'It belonged to my sister. I needed something to store my things in. I felt I had a right to use it, more of a right than Mr Kruger to have it.'

McCleod smiled.

'Don't worry. Of course you had every right to take it with you. Where is it now? Presumably you had to leave it behind with the wagon.'

'Yes. It was too bulky to take with me.'

'Did you take all of the papers that were in the box?'

'Yes. I just scooped them up.'

'Did you look in the box before you left the Cinch Buckle?'

Sandy thought for a moment.

'I don't think so. I was in a hurry to get away. I'd put a few things in a buggy and my papers were the last to be packed. I didn't know where to put them, and then I thought of the box. It was a last minute decision.'

'Was it locked?'

'Yes, but I knew where my sister kept the key.'

'OK. Would you mind if I took a look through your papers?'

McCleod couldn't help but notice a blush which tinged Miss Sandy's features.

'Don't worry. I won't look at what you've written.'

'It's all right,' she said. 'After all, you're about the only person I've ever shown my poems to.'

She passed the bundle to McCleod. It was surprisingly substantial. He began to flick through them and then stopped.

'We don't want to miss anythin',' he said. 'I figure a closer look might be in order.'

Carefully, he and Sandy began to examine the papers, laying them down in a tidy pile as they did so. It soon became obvious to McCleod that they were very disorganized. Apart from the notebooks, which were basically loose sheets of paper bound together with string, there were a lot of miscellaneous cuttings, casual jottings and superfluous items – an illustration from a magazine, a bill for some groceries, a stagecoach ticket. The pile had grown to a considerable size when McCleod came to a creased sheet and, unfolding it, suddenly became more animated. His eyes quickly scanned the page and when he looked up at Miss Sandy and Cherokee there was excitement in his eyes.

'I think we might have found what we're looking

for,' he snapped.

The others regarded him expectantly.

'What is it?' Miss Sandy said.

'Here, take a look for yourself.'

Miss Sandy took the paper and for once even Cherokee George lost his inscrutable expression as he leaned over her shoulder.

'I don't understand,' she said after her eyes had perused it. 'It seems to be written in some sort of legal language. What does it all mean?'

She handed the paper back and McCleod looked it over one more time.

'Well,' he said, 'I ain't no lawyer, but I reckon this document gives your sister legal claim to a lot of property in some place called Prospect.'

'Prospect? Where is that?'

'I ain't too sure, but it looks like it could be somewhere in the hills near Marmot Wallow. Seems to be near some of the old diggings.'

Cherokee looked thoughtful.

'I've heard tell of the place,' he intervened. 'But I don't think anyone's lived there for a long time, not since the gold ran out and they discovered a new field.'

Miss Sandy was looking vague.

'Over that way,' McCleod said, pointing with his finger. 'Me and Cherokee spent a little time in Marmot Wallow on the way to findin' you.'

He looked at Cherokee, remembering the fight at Marmot Wallow. Funny how things sometimes turned out. All their travels seemed to be bringing them back to the place they had set out from.

'But how would my sister have claims to property?'

'Who knows? Did you have much contact with her before you both moved to the Hog Eye?'

'No. I was at school back East. Our parents died when I was very young and I lived with a distant relative, a great-aunt. At that time my sister was livin' with a man called Fogle.'

Suddenly she stopped.

'Fogle! I forgot to mention that I thought I saw a man in Low Butte who looked like him. I couldn't be sure because I never had a lot to do with him.'

'Like I said yesterday, the man who got shot by Kruger's gunnies called himself Fogle. We figure he was someone impersonatin' him.'

McCleod got to his feet and began to pace up and down.

'Fogle,' he said at length. 'I got a feelin' that he's the answer to this little mystery. I'll bet it was Fogle invested in those properties. He probably drew up the agreement in favour of your sister. When your sister left him for Kruger, she took the document with her. She probably never even thought about it. Somehow Kruger didn't get to know about it until she died. Maybe she mentioned somethin' to him. He wasn't sure where she kept the document. By the time he realized it was probably in the box, you had taken it and gone.'

He sat down again.

'Take a look through the rest of those papers yourself, see if there's anythin' else among them belonging to your sister.'

Miss Sandy did so but apart from another old bill and a receipt there was nothing of significance. While she was doing so, McCleod was thinking: where was Fogle now?

'Were you close to your sister?' he asked.

Miss Sandy shook her head.

'Not really. I was surprised when she asked if I wanted to come out West. I was glad to take the opportunity to get away from the boarding school.'

'Well, I guess she had her reasons. We'll never know for sure. Maybe she thought she'd be offering you a stable home at the Hog Eye. Maybe that's one reason she left Fogle for Kruger in the first place.'

Miss Sandy's eyes were suddenly filled with tears.

'Mr McCleod,' she said. 'Do you think my sister died a natural death?'

'That's a strange thing to say,' McCleod replied.

'It's just that, when Mr Kruger began to turn unpleasant, I sometimes wondered. . . .'

'Hey, don't torment yourself,' McCleod replied. He drew Miss Sandy to him and put his arm round her shoulder, glancing at Cherokee as he did so. The man's features were fixed in a fierce glare. McCleod had the impression that there was little doubt in his mind about Kruger's culpability. Miss Sandy soon recovered her composure.

'So, what are we to do now?' she said.

For the first time Cherokee added his voice to the conversation.

'By now,' he said, 'Kruger will know about Miss

Sandy. If he finds that wagon, he'll also find the tin box with nothin' in it. He'll guess what's happened to that document and he won't waste any time tryin' to get his hands on it.'

Miss Sandy looked from Cherokee to McCleod and there was anxiety edged on her features.

'Cherokee's right,' McCleod said. 'We'd best get mounted up and be on our way.'

'But where are we to go?' Miss Sandy said.

'The nearest town, accordin' to your Cinch Buckle man, is Thorpeville. I figure we get there as quickly as possible. You'll be safe there, Miss Sandy, because Kruger will be lookin' for us.'

'How do you work that out?'

'Because me and Cherokee are goin' to head for Marmot Willow to register this document officially and then get on out to Prospect to see what sort of a place it is.'

Miss Sandy considered his proposition.

'I'm sure that's all very reasonable,' she said, 'but you're forgetting a couple of things.'

McCLeod looked puzzled.

'In the first place, I don't want to be left anywhere.'

'It would only be briefly,' McCleod interposed.

'Brief or not, I'm not doing it. Secondly, if what you say is right and my sister owns some property in Prospect, it seems like she wanted to pass them on to me. That means I got a right to go and see the place too. And thirdly, I'm all rigged out for a ride. But more important, I've been running scared of Kruger for too long. I figure it's time I turned the tables on him.'

McCleod and Cherokee exchanged glances.

'The lady's sure got a good point there,' Cherokee said.

McCleod was unconvinced.

'I'll be fine ridin' with you two,' Miss Sandy said. 'Leastways, you'll know exactly where I am.'

'I don't know,' McCleod began.

'Kruger might trail you and Cherokee,' Miss Sandy said, 'but he's not likely to just forget about me. He'll assign one or two of his boys to keep me out of his way. There's no choice. I'll be a lot safer riding with you.'

McCleod could see the sense of her reasoning. It was becoming clear to him that Miss Sandy would never be able to assume she was safe from Kruger until Kruger had been dealt with.

'OK, you win,' he said. 'You can ride with us, but only on condition that you do exactly what we tell you.'

A grin spread across Miss Sandy's face.

'It's a deal,' she replied.

Without waiting around any further, they broke camp, taking care not to leave any obvious traces, and as daylight finally began to flood the hills they set off riding in the direction of Marmot Wallow.

It didn't take Kruger more than a minute to realize that Miss Sandy had escaped his clutches by inches when the Cinch Buckle hand reported what he had seen. Taken with the evidence of the rejected clothing found in the wagon, it was obvious.

'You danged fool,' he shouted. 'Can't you tell the difference between a man and a woman?'

The Cinch Buckle man looked sheepish.

'It were gettin' dark and she was well concealed. Anybody woulda made the same mistake.'

'Get out of my sight.'

Kruger was already annoyed because he had found no trace of Miss Sandy's papers. It hadn't taken Jepson long to find the japanned box but it was empty. Kruger couldn't have expected it to be otherwise, but it still made him furious. He was certain that among those papers was the thing he was looking for; he took some comfort from the fact that it shouldn't be too difficult now to find Miss Sandy. At the very least, he could thank his idiot ranch-hand for having come across her. She was only a matter of miles away. He had a good idea of the direction in which she was headed. It wouldn't be long till they rode her down. His thoughts were interrupted by the sound of laughter. Some of his men were ragging their colleague for his mistake over the gender of Miss Sandy. For the briefest of moments a smile flickered along the edges of his own mouth. It was kinda funny after all. Those boys went a long time without seeing a woman. They would ride miles just to look at a girl. It wasn't surprising if they got out of the habit of even recognizing one.

'Hey Sam!' he shouted. 'Get one of the boys to tell you the difference between a mare and a stallion before we get back to the ranch.'

He could afford a touch of levity. There was nothing in his way now. And if some of his ranch-hands didn't know the difference between a man and a woman, he certainly did; and he intended to let Miss Sandy know it.

McCleod still had doubts about the wisdom of taking Miss Sandy along with them, but there didn't seem to be much choice. Miss Sandy was probably right in saying she would be safer riding with them than if she was left on her own. As safe, at least. A good night's sleep and being with himself and Cherokee seemed to have restored her completely; when he looked at her riding alongside, he could plainly see that she was enjoying herself. The bad weather had finally departed and the sun was shining. They rode hard, wanting to put as much distance between themselves and Kruger as possible. McCleod was beginning to wonder whether he hadn't chosen the wrong option in deciding to wait till morning to take a look at Miss Sandy's papers. If he had done so the day before they would have been able to get further ahead of Kruger. On the other hand, Miss Sandy had needed the time they had spent resting and a decent night's sleep. There was no telling when Kruger would get on their trail but he couldn't be too far behind. Once again McCleod was grateful to have Cherokee along. If there was one man who had the skills and guile to be able to elude any pursuit it was he.

On the second day, towards noon, they halted to

let the horses graze. The land was becoming more arid; Cherokee had noticed bright green patches of loco weed and took care not to let the horses near it. When they resumed their journey, they began to approach a low butte; McCleod speculated that it was maybe the same landmark the town of Low Butte had been named after. It stood more or less in the direction they were headed, the undulating land rising towards it, and only a slight detour would allow them to reach it. McCleod thought it might make a useful lookout point. They reined their mounts and approached the gently rising lower slopes. McCleod was riding in front with Miss Sandy and Cherokee just behind. Suddenly something slithered across the path in front of his horse. The horse reared and at the same moment he heard a loud report from further up the hillside. A bullet went singing past his shoulder. Screaming to the others to do likewise, he threw himself from his rearing horse and they all rolled to the shelter of some nearby rocks, McCleod covering Miss Sandy's body with his own.

'Are you two OK?' he asked.

'I think so,' Miss Sandy replied. 'What happened?'

'Someone up there took a pot shot at me,' McCleod replied. 'It was just pure luck that my horse got spooked.'

Another shot rang out, ricocheting with a snarl from one of the boulders.

'Keep down!' Cherokee barked. From where they were concealed they were quite well covered, but the gunman, whoever he was, had them pinned down.

The horses had fled back down the trail where McCleod hoped they would be out of range. As he was deciding what to do, Cherokee spoke in a low voice.

'I'm going to try and get up behind him. Whatever you do, don't move. Keep your heads down.'

'Wouldn't it be better to stay?' Miss Sandy said.

He shook his head.

'He's got us right where he wants us. We have to do somethin'.'

He slithered away, keeping well in the shelter of the rocks.

'Remember,' he said. 'Don't move.'

Once he was away from the others, he turned over on his back to try and survey the hillside above him. From that angle he could not make out very much. There seemed to be little in the way of cover but some sparse bushes beyond the shelter of the rocks offered a possibility. He had a rough idea of where the shots had come from. He waited to see whether the gunman would fire again, and was rewarded when another shot came smashing into the rocks a little to his left. Shards of stone flew into the air. This time he was able to see a plume of smoke coming from some trees which were just below the summit of the hill. He had a better idea now of just where the gunman had hidden himself. There was a little stretch of fairly open ground between him and the bushes. If he could get across without being hit, or even without the gunman noticing, he might be able to edge round the side of the hill out of sight of their attacker. He debated what would be the best thing to do – make a run for the bushes, or try and crawl on his stomach. The first would catch the man's attention but would be quick. He might accomplish the second without being seen, but if the gunman did spot him he would be an easy target. Still, if he succeeded he would maintain the surprise element. Firing off a shot from behind the boulder to distract the gunman, he crawled into the open.

His stomach felt heavy and cold. He half expected a bullet to come slamming into the small of his back. One thing in his favour was that the grass was fairly long and there wasn't far to go to the shelter of the bushes. Keeping as flat as possible and pushing his gun hand out in front of him, he moved forward. Suddenly he heard shots from the direction of the rocks he had just quitted and he realized that McCleod was firing in order to provide him with some cover. He took advantage of the salvo to crawl forward as quickly as he could and then he was in amongst the bushes.

Doubled over, he began to move around the side of the hill, moving upwards at the same time. The climb was becoming steeper. The shooting seemed to have stopped, then he heard another report but this time more muffled. He had put the shoulder of the hill between himself and his target. More confident now, he made better progress and soon he had reached the top of the butte. Now he needed to be careful. He had to work out as far as he could the gunman's position in relation to where he had come out. He calculated quickly and then began to move across the top of the hill. The tricky part would be to choose the correct spot at which to come down on the gunman. If he got it wrong, he would be exposed against the skyline. He dropped to his stomach again and crawled towards the edge of the hill. Very slowly he raised his head just enough to peer over the rim. He could not see anything because the gunman was directly beneath him. A smile edged its way across his face. The situation was critical, but now he had the upper hand.

There was a drop of about ten feet to where the gunman lay. Quickly he weighed up the options. He might get in a shot but there was a bit of an overhang. If he missed or the gunnie detected him first, he was lost. In an instant he decided what he must do. In one move he rose to his feet and leaped over the edge to hurl himself upon the unsuspecting man beneath. The shock of the impact knocked them both over, the revolver flying out of Cherokee's hand. He was on his feet instantly, and before the gunman had time to react and aim his weapon, Cherokee flung himself forward, crashing into the gunman's stomach and hurling him to the ground. Flinging himself on top of his opponent, he grabbed his gun hand and they fought desperately for possession of the weapon. Cherokee had the better position, and putting out his strength he dashed the man's hand against an outcrop of rock; the gun fell from his grasp and went plummeting down the side of the hill. Grimacing with pain the man succeeded in freeing his wrist and reached up to fasten both his hands around Cherokee's throat. His grip was strong and Cherokee gasped for breath as he sought to dislodge it. The vice-like hands continued to constrict his throat. He felt sick and dizzy. With a desperate effort he brought his fist crashing into the other's face. Blood spurted as the man's nose splattered into a shapeless pulp. His grasp relaxed for a second and Cherokee was able to tear himself free just as a stunning blow from the man's fist sent him rolling over. They were both struggling to their feet but Cherokee was up first to deliver a swinging boot into his opponent's stomach. The shock sent the man reeling backwards to the very edge of the shelf on which they stood, but he managed to gain his balance and as Cherokee came forward he saw something glistening in the man's hand. It was a knife.

'I've got you now,' the bushwhacker hissed.

Cherokee stepped back. The man came forward, the blade in his right hand. He made a move, slashing with the knife. Cherokee jumped aside and for a few moments they circled each other. Again the man stepped forward, jabbing and hacking. Cherokee lurched backwards as the knife sliced through what was left of his shirt front, drawing blood. As they circled, they had exchanged places and now Cherokee stood with his back to the drop.

'You had your chance to kill me,' Cherokee taunted. 'You blew it.'

Enraged, the man rushed forward, but as his knife swung Cherokee deftly stepped aside and grabbed him by the forearm, accelerating his forward rush and swinging him over the edge of the outcrop. With a shriek the man went hurtling down, crashing into the hillside lower down and then tumbling head over heels to lie in a crumpled heap beneath. Exhausted, Cherokee sank to the floor. His throat hurt and blood was flowing from the knife wound in his chest. So far as he could see, though, he was not badly injured. After a few moments he got to his feet and called to the others below. He began to scramble back down the hillside. Towards the bottom he met McCleod and Miss Sandy who were coming towards him.

'You've been hurt!' Miss Sandy exclaimed.

'It ain't nothin' serious,' Cherokee replied. 'Did you see where the man landed?'

'We heard him shout. We were worried for a moment it might be you,' McCleod said.

'Let's go find him. There's somethin' about this I don't understand.' McCleod looked at him.

'You sure you'll be all right?'

'Sure. Come on.'

They climbed back down to the foot of the hill and began to circle round to the spot where the man must have fallen.

'It can't be one of Kruger's men,' Cherokee said.

'That's what I was thinkin',' McCleod replied. 'They couldn't have got this far ahead of us.'

As they came round a corner of the hill they could see the figure of the man lying in the grass. McCleod reached him first and bent down over his prostrate form.

'He's breathin',' he said.

The man was lying on his back. The next moment he moaned and his eyes flickered open. Miss Sandy suddenly gasped.

'Why,' she exclaimed, 'it's Fogle!'

The man had ceased moaning and seemed to be making a recovery. He attempted to sit up but fell back again.

'Take it easy,' McCleod said.

The man lay prone for a few minutes and then made to sit up again. This time he succeeded. He looked around and for the first time saw Miss Sandy. His face immediately broke into a smile of relief and pleasure.

'Miss Sandy!' he gasped.

'Hello, Mr Fogle.'

'I'm so glad I've found you. It's been a long time.'

Struggling to his feet, he stepped forward and embraced her and then, seeing Cherokee George, stepped aside, looking apprehensively at his erstwhile assailant.

'It's OK,' McCleod said. 'But I think you got a few questions to answer.'

They walked slowly back to where they had left the horses and when the man had swallowed a couple of slugs of whiskey he seemed pretty well recovered. The fall had knocked the wind out of him and there were a few cuts and bruises, but he had been lucky to make a soft landing.

'Maybe you'd better start talkin',' McCleod said. 'Why did you take a shot at me? I was plumb lucky you didn't kill me.'

'Yeah, I'm real sorry about that. But I figured you were a couple of Kruger's men. OK, I was way wrong but I'm sure you can understand why I acted the way I did.'

He turned to Cherokee George who, with some reluctance, had been persuaded to let Miss Sandy tend his wound, which wasn't serious.

'No hard feelin's?' he said.

Cherokee George grunted.

'It sure is good to see you,' he continued, addressing Miss Sandy. 'Since I heard about you runnin' away from the ranch, I've been worried out of my mind. I would have tried to reach you earlier but I couldn't do it.'

He looked slightly shamefaced.

'Reason was, I was inside the pen.'

McCleod recalled the marshal's Wanted notice in Low Butte so the revelation came as no surprise.

'I ain't proud of it,' Fogle said, 'but maybe it was a good thing in the end. It made me finally sit up and realize what was happenin' to me.'

'What were you in jail for?' Miss Sandy asked.

'Robbery. Let's just say I got into some bad company. I've put it all behind me now.'

It was a far cry from riding with the Texas Rangers. Briefly, Fogle outlined what had happened to him after Kruger went off with his woman. It was a sorry tale.

'Once I got myself pulled together,' Fogle concluded, 'I decided to come back. I knew Kruger was a bad man, but I'd also been thinkin' about you, Miss Sandy. I came back to try and make amends.'

'You had no reason to make amends,' Miss Sandy replied. 'My leaving school back East to join my sister at the Hog Eye had nothing to do with you.'

'Maybe, but I still felt I owed you somethin'.'

McCleod noticed that he did not mention the death of Sandy's sister. Perhaps the wound of his woman's desertion was still raw. Or maybe he wanted to avoid possibly upsetting Miss Sandy. When he had finished Miss Sandy told him about leaving the Cinch Buckle and what had happened to her recently, but didn't go into too many details about Kruger's behaviour towards her. McCleod filled in the rest of the story.

'So that's Kruger's game!' Fogle snapped when he had finished. He glanced at Miss Sandy. McCleod had the impression he was about to say more but her presence put him under restraint.

'Alicia had a lot of friends,' he said, 'before I knew her. She had a wide social circle. That's how she first came in contact with Kruger. I wasn't interested in her financial affairs, but she had money, I'm sure of that. Quite apart from Kruger's ill-gotten gains from cattle rustlin', I figure he got help from her to help fund his purchases of the Hog Eye and later, the Cinch Buckle.'

He stopped and turned to McCleod.

'You'll let me ride with you?' he said.

McCleod didn't need any time to come to a decision.

'Sure,' he said. 'I reckon you've earned a right to be in at the end of this whole affair.'

'Only make sure you know which side you're on next time,' Cherokee remarked.

Fogle grinned.

'I ain't likely to forget,' he said. 'Not now.'

They rode hard for the next few days. The country grew steadily harsher and more barren as they approached the town of Marmot Wallow. McCleod's initial plan had been to go into the town and see what needed to be done with regard to the legal aspects of the case, but as they got nearer he had a change of plan. Instead of heading into Marmot Wallow, they would ride straight on up into the hills and see if they could locate the settlement of Prospect. In this he was partly influenced by what had happened in Marmot Wallow on the previous occasion he and Cherokee had been there. He didn't want the presence of Cherokee to stir up more trouble. But he had another idea in mind. Cherokee had said he'd heard of the place; McCleod figured it might make a good base. All the time he was aware that Kruger and his gang were not far behind. If they could establish themselves in the town they should be able to put themselves in a more fortified position to meet Kruger when he followed them there. The only question was whether to leave Miss Sandy behind in Marmot Wallow. In the end he decided against it. He had tried weighing up the pros and cons but in the end he gave up. Besides, there was really not much point in using up energy worrying about it. Miss Sandy would never consent to being left behind. The most sensible thing was probably to carry on and make sure she was protected if and when the shooting started.

They rode up into the hills, avoiding the area where the new diggings had opened. Cherokee now led the way. His instincts for finding a place and the best way to it were infallible. Where McCleod would have been floundering, he was able to pick out the narrowest pathways and the disused remnants of old Indian trails. Where there were none, he could still detect the possible ways through. The hills were not high and he had performed far more arduous tasks, not least in his days as a scout in the Civil War. Before long they had their first sighting of their target, the old settlement of Prospect.

Even from a distance, it showed as a more substantial place than McCleod had expected. It wasn't just a collection of abandoned miners' shacks. Instead it was a town of reasonable proportions. McCleod figured it must have been quite a thriving centre in the days when that part of the area had been mined. He didn't know how long ago that had been, but a considerable time must have elapsed before the discovery of gold elsewhere in the range had brought the gold-seekers flooding back. Soon they were approaching the first of the buildings, a few tumble-down shacks with their roofs fallen in. It was obvious that the main drag was losing its battle with the encroaching landscape; grass had grown up and tumbleweed blew about in the evening wind. Weeds poked through the boardwalks. They passed some false-fronted faded buildings that were beginning to lean together. The breeze blew through their empty doors and windows. There was a café, a grocery and dry-goods emporium, a livery stable. They rode on past what appeared to be the marshal's office and jail with bars at the windows, then some other shabby structures that were once saloons and stores. There was even a tiny church whose white paint was now brown, cracked and peeled, and then the street just petered out into the surrounding wilderness. They turned and rode back to what must have once been the biggest saloon, dismounted and tethered their horses to the rickety hitch rail.

'Might as well take a look inside,' McCleod commented.

Miss Sandy took his arm as they mounted the boardwalk and thrust their way through the hanging batwing doors. The place was gloomy and full of dust. Some tables and chairs still stood, others lay on their sides. A roulette wheel had accumulated debris but still remained in the middle of the room. A piano stood abandoned in the corner. Fogle walked over and struck a few keys with his fingers. The out-of-tune notes jangled. Over the bar hung a long cracked mirror which threw back to the intruders their startled features. They wandered back out and began to walk down what had been the main strip towards the church. At the very edge of town was a small graveyard, the few wooden markers lying at odd angles, the rough scrawled writing already indecipherable. The wind was getting stronger now and rippled through the long grass.

'Might as well make ourselves at home,' McCleod said.

'What do you mean?' Miss Sandy replied.

'Well, I reckon we might find us a place for the night back at the saloon.'

They returned to the building. At the side of the bar some broken stairs led up towards a dusky landing. Gingerly they made their way up. At the top there was a dark corridor with peeling wallpaper and several doors hanging open. Quickly they glanced into each of the rooms. Some of them seemed bigger and better preserved than others. In most there was a gimcrack bed and a broken window leading on to a balcony.

'Welcome to our quarters for the night,' McCleod said.

'I think we might have done worse,' Miss Sandy answered, putting on a brave face.

While she began to shake down the beds and sweep away some of the thick dust, McCleod went out on a balcony to take a look over the town. The horses were standing down below and he thought it might be a good idea to check out the livery stable. He and Cherokee untied the horses and led them over to the livery. They hadn't expected there to be much. The stalls were empty and decrepit, but out back there were overgrown corrals which would make decent pasture for the night. They attended to the horses' needs, taking off the saddles and bridles which they left in the barn and taking back their blankets and one or two other items to the saloon. By the time they had made themselves as comfortable as possible, the last of the light had almost gone. They were hungry. In what had been the kitchen they found some old tins of food to supplement their own provisions.

'They should be OK,' McCleod said.

In the end they decided to play safe and eat what provisions they had brought with them. Miss Sandy made coffee. Fogle went behind the bar. A few bottles still remained. He tried to unscrew a bottle of whiskey, but it was unyielding. In the end he knocked it against the bar, rinsed out a couple of glasses and poured them some drinks.

'Let's be thankful for small mercies,' he said.

In the darkness of the deserted saloon they raised their glasses. It was an unusual situation. When they had finished they made their way back up the stairs and sat together on the balcony. The stars hung low and bright over the tumble-down town. The wind soughed.

'What do you think happened here?' Miss Sandy asked McCleod.

'I guess the people left when the ore ran out,' he replied.

Miss Sandy could not sleep that night. The clapboard building groaned and creaked and several times she thought she could hear footsteps on the stairs. The wind moaned and vague menacing noises came to her ears so that she was unsure whether they emanated from outside or from her own imagination. It was a strange thing but she felt almost more vulnerable here than she had done on the open prairie, in spite of the presence nearby of the others. She tried to be rational, but couldn't help feeling nervous. Maybe it was something to do with the fact that people had once lived here. Maybe the buildings bore an imprint of their activities; maybe something of them still haunted the abandoned town. A place like this was aptly named a ghost town. She didn't really believe in ghosts, but she could almost feel their presence here.

McCleod awoke from a brief and fitful slumber convinced that he had heard a footstep on the stair. Being careful not to disturb anyone, he got to his feet and crept silently to the landing. He peered down the dark abyss of the stairwell. He seemed to see shadows, but could discern nothing definite. He began to descend the stairs, being very careful where he put his feet; perhaps one could give way and he might plummet through some hole. He reached the bottom and surveyed the dark enshrouded saloon. Something moved and he swung his gun in its direction. There was a dull thud as whatever it was alighted on one of the piano's dead keys, and then he saw that it was only a cat, some poor, once domesticated animal that had been left behind to fend for itself. He smiled grimly. This place was really getting to him. He picked his way across the floor and through the broken batwings to the boardwalk outside. He felt better to be in the open. He walked to the edge of the dilapidated walkway, and then he tensed. Something fluttered across the ground, something which gleamed very faintly a ghostly white. He could not see what it was, and then the wind blew again and swirled it away. He stepped down to follow and retrieve it. He had lost it again, and then there it was once more, a faint pale object rustling along the ground. He bent and picked it up. It was only a crumpled piece of paper torn from the wall of one of the buildings. Tossing it aside, he was about to make his way back to the saloon when he heard a slight sound like a footfall. He felt annoyed that he had left his six-guns behind but the next moment he relaxed again as the figure of Cherokee emerged from the darkness.

'What are you doin?' McCleod said. 'You might have got yourself shot.'

'You ain't carryin' a gun. Besides, I could say the same thing to you.'

They began to walk slowly down the street.

'I don't like this place,' Cherokee said.

McCleod remembered Cherokee's reaction to making camp anywhere near where Bunce and the man who had called himself Fogle were buried.

'It ain't exactly the sort of place I'd choose to spend a lot of time either,' he replied.

They both felt strange. The place was eerie and the wind blowing through the vacant buildings sounded like the voices of the people who had once lived there come back to visit their old haunts. The dark shapes of the rotting frame structures loomed overhead and seemed to watch through their empty, staring window frames.

'At least we ain't stayin',' McCleod continued. 'How long do you think it'll take till Kruger gets here?'

'He won't be far behind,' Cherokee replied. 'Tomorrow or the day after.'

'Then we'll be ready for him,' McCleod replied.

They turned back in the direction of the hotel and climbed the broken stairs, trying not to make a sound. When McCleod lay down, he could not get back to sleep. He spent the rest of the night tossing and turning, waiting for the dawn and the inevitable arrival of Kruger.

CHAPTER SEVEN

The coming of daylight made everyone feel a lot better. Nobody liked to admit it, but a night in the ghost town had stretched all their nerves. By the time they had eaten breakfast and downed a couple of mugs of coffee, even Cherokee was back to his normal self. McCleod didn't want to waste too much time in getting organized. It wouldn't be long till Kruger and his gang arrived.

'How many do you figure there'll be?' he asked Cherokee and Fogle.

'Quite a few,' Cherokee replied. 'Remember, we were attacked in numbers.'

'From what I know about Kruger and his methods, and from what I've learned, he ain't the kind to take any chances. In a situation like this, where he reckons the stakes are high, he's gonna have plenty of back-up,' Fogle commented.

When they had finished eating, they took a stroll through the town. It looked a lot different in the light of day. Some of the structures were so dilapidated that they felt sure they would be unsafe. McCleod was watching for vantage points but it would be dangerous for anyone to trust the more rickety buildings. One thing he felt pretty sure about; the way they had ridden up through the hills was likely to be the only way in. That was relevant: he intended to hit Kruger with a first barrage of fire as soon as he reached the edge of town. When he got through that, which he would be likely to do given his overwhelming numerical superiority, he would be met by a second and a third volley as he tried to make progress. At the same time as looking for suitable positions, McCleod was checking out ways in and out of the buildings, the amount of cover available, in order to allow himself the maximum degree of flexibility. Once he or Cherokee or Fogle had loosed their bullets, it was important that they move, change position and continue the fight from a new vantage point. The route that each of them was to follow needed to be carefully planned out, checked and co-ordinated. Ammunition needed to be stacked and available. And not least, there was the question of where was the safest place for Miss Sandy to stay. When he broached the subject, however, she made it plain that she had no intention of removing herself from the struggle.

'I haven't come all this way to sit by and do nothing,' she said. 'I can handle a gun. In fact, I'm a very good shot.'

'I don't doubt it,' McCleod replied, 'but this ain't no business for a woman.'

'It's every bit my business. Especially bearing in mind everything that I now know about Mr Kruger.'

McCleod looked to Cherokee and Fogle for support but both of them looked blank.

'If what you say about Mr Kruger is correct, you're going to need all the help you can get.'

For some reason, McCleod recalled a previous conversation he had had with Cherokee. He had called Miss Sandy a child but Cherokee had called her a woman. Maybe, after all that had happened to her recently, and the way she had been forced to handle her difficulties, she was more of a woman than he was giving her credit for. The girl he had known in the past was still there, but he maybe he had underestimated how she had grown.

'OK,' he said. 'Guess we should have left you behind in Marmot Wallow if we'd thought more about all this. Maybe it's too late for that now. But make sure you don't take any unnecessary risks and follow instructions.'

By the end of the morning they were prepared and ready to take up their posts. McCleod was positioned on the roof of a store. Cherokee had selected a place on the lower floor of a two-storey building on the opposite side, and a little further down Fogle was stationed on the balcony of the hotel. Miss Sandy remained in her bedroom, from the window of which she could fire and lend support to Fogle. The arrangement suited McCleod. When Fogle had appeared on the scene he thought there might be some degree of awkwardness between him and Miss

Sandy, but that hadn't happened. Instead, they seemed to get on well. It was true that Miss Sandy had had little contact with Fogle in the days when he was with her sister, but their separate relationships with that woman seemed to bind them together. McCleod had confidence in Fogle to look out for Miss Sandy. They gathered together in the bar of the saloon to eat their lunch.

'Everyone know what they have to do?' McCleod checked.

They all nodded.

'Sure thing. I just want Kruger to get here,' Fogle said.

McCleod looked closely at Miss Sandy.

'You still sure about this?' he said.

'Don't worry about me. I feel the same way as Mr Fogle.'

It was certainly true that she appeared to exhibit no sense of trepidation or nerves. Could she be the same girl he had once known? He had only to think of the strength and resourcefulness she had shown to realize that she had attained to womanhood.

'OK. Let's get into position.'

Fogle and Miss Sandy climbed the stairs to the upper floor of the saloon. McCleod and Cherokee walked down the overgrown street. When they were all in position McCleod signalled from his rooftop and the signal was returned. He could see them and they could see him. Sitting down and resting his back against a balustrade, he pulled out his tobacco pouch and rolled himself a cigarette.

The minutes passed into hours and the hours ticked by. The number of cigarette stubs multiplied. The sun, having climbed to its zenith, began to inch its way down the sky. A cooling breeze blew down from the peaks carrying the freshness of pine needles. It was hard to believe that they were no more than a few days' riding from the harshness and heat of the badlands. Looking over the edge of the parapet, McCleod had a good view of the surrounding country and the approach to the town. It was a spectacular prospect but its magnificence was wasted on him. Behind the town the hills rose high without ever becoming mountainous. Trees lined their slopes and he guessed that somewhere in their depths the old mines were located. From time to time he stood up and waved his arm to check that the others were watching. He had just done so for the third or fourth time – he had lost track – when he saw something move a long way down the slope of the hillside. There was a glint of light. He put his field glasses to his eyes. A column of riders had appeared round a corner of the hill. Kruger! He remained standing and signalled again, this time the prearranged signal that told the others that Kruger had arrived. Once the signal was returned he kneeled down and watched the approach of the riders. There were more of them than he had bargained for; he counted fifteen and there was no knowing whether there might be others coming along further behind. For a few moments he had second thoughts about the wisdom of meeting Kruger here in this deserted spot.

Maybe he had got it all wrong. But he knew that sooner or later they would have to face the menace and now was as good a time as any. At least he had chosen the scene of action. That was their big advantage. He recalled a number of times when taking the initiative had proved vital in the War Between the States. It had meant the difference between success and failure, life and death, and there was no reason to suppose that it would be any different this time. His one real regret was that he had listened to Miss Sandy. This was not the place for her to be and he should have obeyed his own instincts and left her behind either in Thorpeville or in Marmot Wallow. There was nothing he could do about that now.

He continued to observe the column of riders. Slowly but inexorably it was climbing the long slope leading to the ruined town. At the top the climb levelled off for a considerable stretch before the first outlying shacks were reached. He raised his Winchester to his shoulder and sighted it. He had already worked out the exact moment when he would open fire. It was just a question of waiting till Kruger reached the spot. He licked his lips. The column had just crested the slope and some of the riders were beginning to bunch together. For a few moments they halted and one of them began pointing ahead. A couple of others reined in alongside and the group became involved in discussion. Had they spotted something? McCleod glanced back along the street below him but he could detect nothing that might give them away. Cherokee and

Fogle were well concealed. Had one of the horses in the livery stable made a noise which they could have detected? Kruger and his men and horses were making sufficient noise themselves. Further reflection was ended when the column began to move forward again. Some of the front riders had pulled their rifles from their scabbards and were holding them loosely. McCleod was looking out for Kruger but he couldn't see him. It had been a long time since he had worked on the Hog Eye so it wasn't surprising. Kruger had probably changed quite a bit in that time. They all had.

Suddenly the group of riders came to a halt again. Some of them were looking confused and others were turning towards one another. McCleod became aware of something happening on the street and swung his head to see what it was. Instantly he gasped and almost jumped to his feet. Coming along the street towards him was the slight figure of Miss Sandy. She was walking slowly but steadily, looking neither to the left nor the right. There was movement among the riders and then from among their ranks a horse spurred forward. Those in the front parted ranks to let him through and one of them moved forward to join him, riding close behind. Although he could not see him very clearly, McCleod knew it was Kruger. Kruger rode past the spot which McCleod had chosen for his opening salvo and carried on till he was almost opposite to where he crouched behind the coping of the roof of the building. He looked sideways. Miss Sandy had reached to within a matter of yards to where Kruger had drawn rein. Her expression was firm and determined and she showed no sign of being afraid. Behind Kruger, the other riders had drawn close. Tension hung in the air. McCleod for once was at a loss what to do. All he could do was watch what was happening and hope that the unfolding drama would not result in catastrophe for Miss Sandy. For what seemed long minutes Kruger and Miss Sandy confronted one another without either saying anything. In fact it was only a matter of moments before Miss Sandy spoke, her voice ringing clear and loud above the pregnant silence which had descended over the scene.

'Mr Kruger,' she began. 'I know why you are here. I know why you have been so persistent in following me all this time, and I don't care. All I want to do is to avoid any further trouble or bloodshed. All I want is for you to leave me alone.'

Kruger leaned over the pommel of his horse.

'You say you know why I'm here. Then you know more than I do, lady,' he said.

Miss Sandy suddenly laughed.

'Take a look around you,' she said. 'This is what it's all been about. Take it, it's yours. But just get your men to put their guns away.'

She suddenly reached into a pocket of her dress and produced the document assigning her sister the property in Prospect.

'Here, this is what you've been looking for. Go ahead, read it. That's the document my sister put away in her chest. I didn't know anything about it till recently. I admit I took the box but I never knew there was anything in it. I just wanted somewhere to keep my papers when I left the Cinch Buckle.'

Even from his advantage point, McCleod could see that Kruger was uncomfortable. The last thing he would want his men to know would be details of the reasons behind Miss Sandy's decision to leave the Cinch Buckle. Miss Sandy approached his horse to hand over the document and he began to read it. It didn't take him long.

'There must be some mistake,' he said.

'There's no mistake. Look all about you. It belongs to you. I relinquish any claim to it. This place is yours. This is what you've been plotting and scheming for.'

As if in answer to her invitation, Kruger looked all about him at the falling, crumbling shell of what had once been a thriving settlement. He raised himself in the saddle and, partly turning, peered back at his men. The one who had ridden up beside him leaned across.

'What's the problem?' he said.

Suddenly, Kruger began to laugh, but not like Miss Sandy. Beginning gently, it rapidly swelled in volume till it rang out almost hysterically. The sound of his laughter was oddly disturbing in the quiet afternoon in the empty, weed-filled street. His men looked at one another questioningly and a few broke into uncertain, broken chuckles.

'Look at this place, Jepson! Look at it!' Kruger managed to say.

Suddenly he calmed down and the next moment

he had reached for his rifle.

'You won't make a fool of me!' he gasped.

Miss Sandy stepped back. At the same moment McCleod got to his feet and stood above the scene, his rifle pointing at Kruger.

'Don't do anything stupid, Kruger!' he snapped.

Kruger swung his head.

'I wondered when you would show up!' he snarled. 'I don't know who you are but you've made a big mistake gettin' involved in this.'

Before McCleod could reply another voice called out from across the street.

'Better put your weapon down, Kruger! We got you and your men covered!'

Kruger broke into a manic laugh again as he turned his rifle back towards Miss Sandy.

'You got this all wrong!' he shouted. 'I figure you'd better come on out or the girl dies!'

McCleod's eyes flickered to the rest of the riders, detecting a restlessness that was spreading through their ranks. There was a strange timelessness about the situation, as if the ghost town lived in its own atmosphere of a separate and vanished age. Things seemed to move slowly and when he saw Miss Sandy begin to walk away from Kruger there was an air of unreality about it.

'Where the hell are you going!' Kruger snapped. 'Stop right where you are or I'll blow a hole straight through you!'

Miss Sandy continued walking, unmoved by his threat.

'You hear what I'm sayin'? Get back here. Now!'

Miss Sandy kept walking. McCleod realized that Kruger had got himself into a fix. If he actually shot the girl it was doubtful that his men would find it acceptable. They might be tough and have few scruples, but it was the unwritten code of the West that a woman was inviolable. There was already some murmuring and Kruger seemed to sense the dissension that he was in danger of arousing. McCleod continued to stand with his rifle trained on Kruger. He had one eye on the rancher and the other on the progress of Miss Sandy as she continued to make her way back towards the saloon. He calculated that she must be almost there when suddenly a shot rang out. McCleod turned in the direction from which the shot had come. At the same moment Kruger wheeled his horse and, almost colliding with Jepson in the process, began to ride back in the direction he had come from. McCleod hit the deck as sporadic shooting became a concentrated volley of fire. Kruger's men were in a state of confusion. The rapid fire, coupled with the impact of Kruger's horse pounding past them, caused some of their horses to rear and others to back into the ones behind. McCleod raised his head a fraction above the parapet. Bullets were thudding into the wood and brickwork but most of them were flying over his head. In that moment he had time to see Kruger's men running in all directions for shelter from a hail of bullets which was issuing from the building across the way where Cherokee was stationed. He had no way of telling whether Miss Sandy had made it back to the shelter of the saloon and he had no time to think about it. He was seeing the disadvantages of his position. If he had been able to fire first the situation would have been a lot different, but as it was he was pinned down. The Cinch Buckle men knew he was positioned there and it was mainly the angle at which they were having to fire that rendered most of their shots useless and was serving to save his skin. It could not last for long. Once they had found suitable positions, their fire-power would be more accurate and he couldn't hope to remain long unscathed. He needed to act, and quickly.

Keeping low, he moved to the opposite side of the roof, the side facing away from the main street. He slung his rifle around his shoulders. The noise of firing was ferocious behind him but when he glanced over the edge of the parapet he could see that so far none of Kruger's men had reached the alley below. He knew the main danger would come when he raised himself up so he braced himself to do it as quickly as possible. Poised on his toes, he sprang to the top of the parapet and almost in the same movement, swung his legs over. It was a good drop to the ground. For just a moment he hung by his hands and then he let go. He hit the ground with a jarring thud and fell backwards to one side. He felt a pain in his leg and blood was oozing from the back of one hand where he had scraped it, but in a moment he was on his feet and running parallel to the main street in the direction of the saloon where he had left Fogle. As he ran he felt the whine of a bullet and heard the report of a gun behind him. He dodged and weaved to make himself a harder target but in a moment he had come to the narrow passageway alongside the saloon and ducked down it. He emerged on to the main street. A glance was enough to show him that the Cinch Buckle men must have split up and found shelter in the nearest buildings. A number of them lay sprawled on the ground and a grim smile twitched the corners of his mouth as he thought of Cherokee. Shots were coming from above him and he guessed it was Fogle firing down the street from the balcony. In case Fogle thought he was one of Kruger's men he shouted up to him and then ran through the broken batwings into the saloon, coming to an immediate halt. Now his fears hit him. He hadn't had time to think too closely about Miss Sandy and whether she had made it to safety. Now he was faced with the immediate prospect of knowing the truth. He was almost afraid to move any further when Sandy herself appeared at the top of the stairs.

'Mr McCleod!' she gasped and came running down the stairs towards him. He sprang forward and they met halfway up.

'Are you OK?' he said.

'Yes.'

Before he could say anything else the figure of Fogle appeared.

'I tried to stop her,' he said, 'but she was too quick for me.'

McCleod looked down at her. She was shaking and

trembling. The strain of it all had caught up with her.

'It was a foolish thing to do,' he said. 'You could easily have got yourself killed.'

'I know that now, but I felt I had to do something to stop the shooting.'

'It was very brave too,' McCleod said.

He looked up at Fogle.

'Can you see much of what's happenin'?' he asked.

'Yeah. Kruger's boys got into a bit of a mess. Some of 'em rode off but most of 'em jumped down from their horses and sought the nearest shelter. I did my best to keep Miss Sandy covered. Your friend Cherokee seems to have pinned quite a few of 'em down, but I figure we need to do somethin' about reinforcin' him.'

McCleod took Miss Sandy by the shoulders.

'Listen,' he said. 'Fogle and me need to get back into the action. You must stay here. But don't try anything this time. Do you hear? Just wait and keep your head down.'

'I will,' she replied. 'But you can't stop me using my rifle if I can get a decent shot in.'

'I thought you wanted to stop this?' McCleod replied.

'I did,' she said. 'I know I didn't do as you asked and maybe that was wrong of me, but I would do it again if I thought it might work. It's too late now though. That chance has passed.'

McCleod glanced up at Fogle.

'Come on, he snapped. 'We ain't got no time to lose.'

They ran out into the street and then began to move along it, keeping close to the walls of the buildings. They hadn't got far when shots began to ping all around. Kruger's men had obviously caught sight of them. They fired back but both of them realized their shots were ineffective. McCleod ducked through the nearest doorway, pulling Fogle after him. He ran through the empty shell of the structure and crashed through the back door. They were in the alley down which McCleod had fled. He paused long enough to see whether the man who had shot at him was still there but he must have returned to the fray.

'Cherokee can't hold out much longer by himself,' McCleod said. 'I'm goin' back to try and work my way down to him. If you carry on here you should be out of the line of fire. When you get towards the end, take up a position in one of the buildings, but be careful none of Kruger's boys has got in there before you.'

'You'll be takin' a big risk,' Fogle said.

'I'll be all right. Just get into a position where you can draw a bead on some of the varmints.'

Fogle nodded and without waiting further McCleod passed through the empty building and stopped at the entrance-way. Now was the most dangerous moment. He needed to cross to the opposite side of the street. He reckoned that when he stepped out he might have a few moments before Kruger's boys opened fire on him; unless they were keeping their guns trained on the spot. Taking a deep breath and holding his rifle at arm's length, he sprinted out into the open. For the first few strides there was no response and then a cacophony of gunfire sounded from the buildings lower down and bullets kicked up dirt nearby. He was already halfway across when he suddenly went tumbling. Although he registered no pain he assumed he had been hit. His momentum carried him almost to the other side and even as he crashed to the ground he had the presence of mind to roll forward so that he was in the shelter of the nearest building. For a moment he lay drawing breath as he realized that he was unscathed apart from a few minor bruises caused by his fall. A bullet thudded into the wooden framework above his head but the next second he was on his feet and crashing through the door into the building. He figured to do the same thing he had told Fogle to do – go straight through and out the back where he might be able to make his way down to where Cherokee was stationed. He ran through and pitched himself at the back door but this time it did not answer to his charge. He kicked at the door but it seemed to be wedged shut. He took a glance about him; the window frames yawned wide and he quickly climbed through.

The town consisted almost entirely of the one street and he found himself in an overgrown yard running down to a level stretch beyond which the ground sloped to the surrounding hills. To his right was the livery stable where their horses were housed. He began to walk quickly away from the livery stable when there was a resounding crash and he felt a searing pain high on his shoulder which caused him to drop the rifle. He fell to his knees as another bullet slapped into the wall where he had been standing. He rolled over, drawing his six-gun, as a further shot rang out and a bullet struck him high in the fleshy part of his thigh. This time he had spotted the stab of flame coming from higher up the slope where a clump of bushes concealed his attacker. He returned fire as another crashing boom delivered a bullet which whistled by his ear. He realized now that whoever it was on the hillside had him plumb in his sights and there was nowhere he could run. Whatever weapon the man was firing, it carried a heavy weight of lead. Thinking rapidly, he decided that there was only one very slim chance of staying alive, and that was by playing possum. As another shot roared its message of death he flung out his hands and slumped to the ground, trying as he did so to stay within the shadow of the building and make himself as small a target as possible. At the same time, he kept his hand on the trigger of his six-gun, ready to fire should his attacker reveal himself. His spine was tingling and he felt a sickening hollow sensation in the pit of his stomach. He had no way of knowing how bad he had been hit but the wound to his shoulder in particular was hurting badly.

Even as he lay there he could hear the continuing sounds of shooting in the street beyond and he felt a sense of guilt. Most of the fighting seemed to have fallen to Cherokee. He could only hope that Fogle had found a good place from which to lend his support because it didn't look like he was going to be able to do much to help. He became aware that someone had emerged from the bushes and was coming down the slope. He turned his head very slightly; after what seemed an eternity the lower half of a figure came into his view. It came closer, moving silently on the grass. Then a voice, strangely high-pitched, rang out.

'Take your hand away from that gun!'

For a fraction of a second McCleod considered trying to swivel and shoot but he realized it was no good. He would be blown to pieces before he had moved an inch. His hand twitched and the six-gun slid away.

'You and your friends have put me to a lot of inconvenience,' the voice continued.

McCleod lay still. His brain was trying to think but a huge tiredness seemed to have come over him.

'Turn over!' the voice rapped.

Wincing with pain, McCleod did as he was ordered. He could see the man now and even after all the time that had elapsed since he had last seen him, he recognized Kruger. Kruger approached close and brought his rifle down to within an inch of McCleod's face.

'Who are you?' he said.

'What's it to you, Kruger?'

For a moment Kruger hesitated, then a look of rage spread over his features; lifting the rifle, he smashed the butt into McCleod's stomach. A wave of nausea and pain spread through McCleod's body as he braced himself for the shot he expected to come next. Instead, through the mists of pain, he thought he heard another voice.

'Kruger! I wouldn't do anythin' more. Throw away your gun or I'll blow you clear through that wall!'

McCleod opened his eyes and looked beyond Kruger. Standing further off was Fogle. He looked up at Kruger.

'I'd do as he says if I were you!' he managed to gasp.

'Do it! Now!' Fogle called.

Kruger hesitated for just a moment longer. A shot rang out loud and clear and a bullet went crashing into the wall of the building.

'The next one's for you!'

Kruger had shrunk at the report and his face was blanched. With a despairing gesture he threw his rifle to the ground. In another moment Fogle had come up.

'McCleod, are you hurt bad?' he asked.

McCleod managed to summon a wan smile.

'Not as bad as I would have been if you hadn't showed up.'

Slowly and painfully he got to his feet. He became aware again of shots ringing out from beyond the line of buildings but they seemed to have become more sporadic.

'I think your boys have just about had enough,' Fogle said to Kruger. 'Once they see you and we explain how you were tryin' to get away, I think they'll see the sense of callin' it a day.'

He turned to McCleod.

'Can you manage?'

'Sure. Lead the way.'

Fogle pressed his rifle into Kruger's back.

'Start walkin',' he ordered. 'And keep your hands in the air.'

They started to move down the line of the buildings parallel to the main street. By the time they had reached a connecting passageway the sound of shooting had almost ceased.

'You go first,' Fogle snapped.

Kruger half turned to him.

'You can't make me do that! Someone will take a shot at me.'

'They might. They might not. That's just a chance you're gonna have to take.'

He prodded the rifle into Kruger's back. Kruger was visibly shaking. He took a step forwards and then halted again.

'Go on. Another step or two.'

Kruger began to plead. Fogle slipped by him.

'Hold your fire!' he shouted. 'I got Kruger!'

The desultory firing ceased. A palpable silence fell over the deserted town like dust. Then a voice called.

'Let's see him!'

Fogle turned to Kruger.

'OK,' he said. 'You heard the man.'

Kruger was still reluctant. Finally Fogle and McCleod seized hold of him and stepped out into the street. Suddenly Kruger wrenched himself free and stumbled clear.

'Shoot them!' he shouted. 'Go on. Shoot them!'

McCleod glanced up the street, his eyes searching the buildings.

'What are you waitin' for?' Kruger screamed.

From the doorway of a building higher up on the opposite side a figure stepped out into the street.

'What happened to you, Kruger!' he shouted.

'Jepson! I order you to shoot!' Kruger shouted.

Jepson moved forward. Kruger looked from him to Fogle and McCleod and suddenly began to run. Jepson pulled out his gun and fired into the air.

'Stop right there!' he shouted.

Kruger kept going.

'Let him go,' McCleod said as Jepson came closer. 'There ain't nowhere for him to run.'

Jepson looked from McCleod to Fogle.

'He was tryin' to get away when I caught up with him,' Fogle said. 'He made the mistake of stopping to bushwhack McCleod.'

'Don't look like he was too successful,' Jepson said.

They looked up the street. Kruger was almost at the end when a figure stepped out of an alleyway in front of him.

'Cherokee!' McCleod said.

Kruger came to a halt. He turned as if to run back and then sank to his knees.

'Looks like that's as far as he's gonna get,' Jepson said.

He was thoughtful for a moment before turning to Fogle and McCleod.

'In fact, I'd say this whole thing has just about gone far enough,' he said. 'Guess none of us realized till now just what Kruger's game was.'

As the Cinch Buckle men began to emerge from their places of concealment, Jepson, McCleod and Fogle walked towards Cherokee. Kruger had begun to sob uncontrollably.

'What do we do with him?' Jepson said.

McCleod looked to the others. He was thinking hard. Kruger had a lot to answer for, not least the killings of the sham Fogle and Bunce. But could anything be proved? And what might it mean for Miss Sandy? It wouldn't be good for her to get involved in the fallout. And what about the rest of the Cinch Buckle outfit? Seeing Kruger grovelling in the dirt, knowing that he had tried to run out on them, they weren't in any mood to go easy on him. They had lost a number of men in the battle which had taken place. Maybe it was time to draw a line under the whole thing.

'Give him a horse,' McCleod said.

Kruger looked anxious.

'Don't worry, there ain't gonna be any lynchin's,' McCleod said.

When a horse had been produced, Kruger was helped into the saddle.

'You OK with this?' McCleod said to Fogle. 'You're the one with the biggest grudge.'

'Yeah. I'm just glad things turned out OK and we found Miss Sandy,' Fogle replied.

'Start ridin',' McCleod said, 'and make sure you don't show your face to any of us again. And keep away from the Cinch Buckle.'

Kruger didn't show any inclination to argue the case. McCleod slapped the rump of the horse and it went off down the street. The little crowd watched it as it dwindled into the distance. As it vanished round a turn in the trail McCleod wobbled.

'Hell, I almost forgot,' Fogle said, 'he's been wounded. Best get him inside.'

Jepson turned to his men.

'We got some casualties of our own to see to,' he said.

That night the old ghost town seemed almost restored, at least in part, to its former self. Light spilled from the saloon and voices drifted on the night air. They were the voices of McCleod, Cherokee, Fogle and Miss Sandy. They were gathered round a fire, having just eaten. Miss Sandy had done a pretty good job of patching up McCleod's injuries and he lay on some blankets, feeling a lot better. Jepson and the rest of the Cinch Buckle boys had left to make their way back to the ranch.

'What'll happen to the Cinch Buckle?' Fogle said.

'If he's got any sense, Kruger will keep well away,' Cherokee replied.

'You know, I got a hunch that when we look at your sister's papers in more detail,' McCleod said, 'we might well find that Kruger never owned either the Cinch Buckle or the Hog Eye. I figure it probably ain't just this old place that rightfully belongs in her name.'

Miss Sandy sighed.

'I don't care,' she said. 'Once I've got Concho, I

never want to go back to the Cinch Buckle again.'

'Well, I guess I can understand that,' Fogle replied, 'but what do you plan on doin'?'

Miss Sandy shook her head.

'You're all the family I got now,' she said.

Fogle smiled.

'I was hopin' you'd say that. I got plans to settle down, maybe open a little store. You wouldn't consider—'

Miss Sandy flung her arms round his neck.

'Oh yes. Now that you've come back, I don't want to lose you again.'

She turned to McCleod and Cherokee.

'And you must come and visit,' she said. 'Wherever it is.'

McCleod adjusted his position slightly to relieve pressure on his injured shoulder.

'Just so long as it ain't in Prospect,' he replied.

Miss Sandy seemed excited by her vision of the future.

'I want to write,' she said. 'Maybe I could enrol on a course in college. There's so much I want to do.'

She turned to McCleod.

'Maybe I can put you and Cherokee in a poem?' she said.

McCleod and Cherokee exchanged glances. From somewhere outside a night-bird called.

'Just make sure it rhymes,' McCleod replied.